T0311235

"This classic has refreshed my spirit time and again when my soul has longed for Christ-centered guidance through a maze of modern detours and diversions. I'm so grateful this special edition of *The Pilgrim's Progress* is now available to not only a new generation of Christians but to believers like myself who need direction and refreshment along our journey toward Home."

> JONI EARECKSON TADA, President, Joni and Friends International Disability Center

"If any smoothing of Bunyan's seventeenth-century language plus new colored pictures can set *Pilgrim's Progress* aglow in the hearts of today's young readers, this lovely book will surely do it."

> J. I. PACKER, Professor of Theology, Regent College

"Every generation is heir to John Bunyan's timeless allegory, and to each generation falls the task of commending this tale anew. The collaboration of editor C. J. Lovik and illustrator Mike Wimmer has yielded a book that could well be a classic for our time. With great care, Lovik has combined the best elements of Bunyan's rich, evocative prose with accessibility for the modern reader. And in Wimmer, Bunyan has met his illustrator for the twenty-first century. The thirty illustrations that grace this edition are a world in themselves—the equal of any that appear in J.R.R. Tolkien's books."

> KEVIN BELMONTE, lead historical consultant for the motion picture *Amazing Grace*

"If you are looking for a classic edition of *The Pilgrim's Progress*, with a simplified form of Bunyan's original text, traditional color illustrations, and explanatory notes, this is undoubtedly the version for you."

> TIMOTHY DOWLEY, author of *The Christians*

"For two centuries following its publication (Part 1 in 1678, Part 2 in 1684), *The Pilgrim's Progress* gained the status of best-read book (apart from the Bible). This magnificent production by Crossway with stunning illustrations by Mike Wimmer should help reinstate Bunyan's classic allegory to the status it belongs. It should be a question we ask ourselves: Have I read *The Pilgrim's Progress*? If not, repent immediately, for in taking up this volume you will find pastoral insights from a pastor of souls to help you discover the biblical way of salvation and aid you in the journey home."

> DEREK W. H. THOMAS, John E. Richards Professor of Systematic Theology, Reformed Theological Seminary (Jackson)

"This is one of the best books I've ever read."

> MARK DEVER, Senior Pastor, Capitol Hill Baptist Church

"C. J. Lovik's new edition of *The Pilgrim's Progress* almost takes one's breath away. The text is readable, the notes are clear, and the illustrations are absolutely beautiful. This is a book to be in everyone's library and will definitely occupy a prominent place in the libraries provided for Rafiki's children and adults in Africa. It is a joy to know that Lovik's edition of the Bunyan classic will be read by and to thousands of children throughout the world."

ROSEMARY JENSEN, Founder and President, Rafiki Foundation; author of *Praying the Attributes of God* and *Living the Words of Jesus*

"*The Pilgrim's Progress* has long been a favorite of many. Now there is even more to love with this beautiful, updated edition. Editor's notes clarify the ideas in John Bunyan's classic allegory, while footnotes show where in Scripture Bunyan found them. The detailed color illustrations will delight both new readers and long-time lovers of this beloved tale."

STARR MEADE, author of *Keeping Holiday* and *Training Hearts, Teaching Minds*

"Like countless others, I have been greatly influenced by *The Pilgrim's Progress*. Charles Spurgeon called it 'next to the Bible, the book that I value most.' It has already inspired generations, and I am confident that this new edition will inspire the rising generation. It is refreshingly readable while remaining true to this timeless classic. The illustrations, Scripture references, and study notes make it a superb resource for family devotions and study groups."

SUSAN HUNT, author of *Spiritual Mothering*

"The longer I journey through our dear Immanuel's land, the more grateful I am for John Bunyan's 'dream' and the cruel imprisonment that occasioned it. What a gift weary travelers have been given in this precious, timeless classic—and what beauty, insight, and encouragement was borne out of his suffering! Unafraid to challenge the outward trials of moralism, materialism, and persecution, humble enough to confess his own doubts and despair, Bunyan leads us on our way to the Celestial City we long to see. And what a gift modern readers have been blessed with in C. J. Lovik's careful editing and Mike Wimmer's luminous illustrations! This book is beautiful! *The Pilgrim's Progress* has always been a cherished treasure, but this edition makes Christian's story—our story—sing! I'm so thankful for it!"

ELYSE FITZPATRICK, author of *Because He Loves Me* and *Comforts from the Cross*

"If a picture truly does speak a thousand words, this version of *The Pilgrim's Progress* will be the best of all. Combining the beauty of Mike Wimmer's illustrations with this timeless classic is a stroke of genius."

STEVE MURPHY, Publisher, *Homeschooling Today* magazine

The Pilgrim's Progress

The Pilgrim's Progress

From This World to
That Which Is to Come

John Bunyan

C. J. Lovik, editor
Illustrated by Mike Wimmer

CROSSWAY®

WHEATON, ILLINOIS

The Pilgrim's Progress: From This World to That Which Is to Come

Updated text copyright © 2009 by C. J. Lovik

Illustrations copyright © 2009 by C. J. Lovik

Published by Crossway
          1300 Crescent Street
          Wheaton, Illinois 60187

Cover design: Tyler Deeb, Misc. Goods Co.

Cover and interior illustrations: Mike Wimmer

First printing 2009

Reprinted with new cover 2019

Printed in China

Hardcover ISBN: 978-1-4335-6250-1
PDF ISBN: 978-1-4335-0700-7
Mobipocket ISBN: 978-1-4335-0701-4
ePub ISBN: 978-1-4335-1880-5

Library of Congress Cataloging-in-Publication Data

Bunyan, John, 1628–1688.
   The pilgrim's progress : from this world to that which is to come /
John Bunyan ; updated by C.J. Lovik ; illustrated by Michael Wimmer.
— (Updated version).
      p. cm.
   Includes bibliographical references.
   ISBN-13: 978-1-4335-0699-4 (hc)
   1. Christian pilgrims and pilgrimages—Fiction. 2. Christian life—
Fiction. I. Lovik, Craig John, 1946–   . II. Title.
PR3330.A2L68   2009
823'.4—dc22   2009004765

Crossway is a publishing ministry of Good News Publishers.

RRD		29	28	27	26	25	24
13	12	11	10	9	8	7	6	5	4

Contents

LIST OF ILLUSTRATIONS

Publisher's Foreword

The Bunyan Legacy

Except for the Bible itself, *The Pilgrim's Progress* is widely recognized as the most influential, beloved, and widely distributed book in the English language. First published in 1678, it became instantly popular throughout English culture, irrespective of education, economic status, or social class. It is widely regarded as a work of genius, though the author, John Bunyan (1628–1688), had only a limited, grade-school education and made his living at the tinker's trade, going from house to house repairing pots and pans.

Bunyan's achievement is all the more remarkable, given the fact that he was the object of extended religious persecution as a result of his call to preaching. From 1655 to 1660, Bunyan preached regularly at the local Bedford Baptist congregation and in the surrounding towns. But because he had not been licensed to preach by the established Church of England, he was imprisoned in the primitive conditions of the Bedford Jail beginning in early 1661, where he languished for the next twelve years. It is during this period, however, that Bunyan most likely wrote the original draft of *The Pilgrim's Progress*, with a copy of the Bible providing his only reference material.

Written in the form of a highly imaginative allegory, *The Pilgrim's Progress* tells the unforgettable story of Christian and the extreme, soul-threatening dangers he encounters on his journey to the Celestial City. But it is also much more than an allegory; in a sense, it is both the personal story of Bunyan and the universal story of anyone who undertakes the same eternal pilgrimage. The result is a masterpiece of literature as well as spiritual truth—a book that at one time was loved and read in nearly every home in England and North America, a book that has endured as a classic for more than three centuries.

ABOUT THIS EDITION

The purpose in publishing this edition of *The Pilgrim's Progress* is to carry forward this treasured legacy for a new generation. With this as the objective, the text of this edition has only been lightly edited. Thus the intention of both the editor and the publisher has only been to update highly archaic words and awkward sentence structure, while retaining the beauty and brilliance of the original story. Likewise, the intention of this edition has never been to simplify or to change Bunyan's original story, but to let the story unfold with all the power, truth, and remarkable creativity of the original. It is our hope and prayer, then, that the following pages will fascinate and captivate the hearts and minds of this generation today, as was the case when *The Pilgrim's Progress* was first published more than three centuries ago.

It should be noted further that this new edition has become a reality only through the vision of the editor, C. J. Lovik. As the publisher of this edition we are deeply grateful to Mr. Lovik—for his lifelong love, from the age of nine, for John Bunyan and *The Pilgrim's Progress*; for his literary skill and great care in editing the text; and for his painstaking labor of love in doing the editorial work over more than a decade. It is indeed a privilege to be entrusted with the publication of *The Pilgrim's Progress*, which we seek to carry out in a manner worthy of Bunyan's legacy.

Lastly, it is important to note the new art that was created specifically for this edition—the thirty, full-color, original paintings by the highly acclaimed artist, Mike Wimmer, which appear throughout the following pages. There is a sense in which these new paintings also carry forward the Bunyan legacy, in that many of the earliest editions of *The Pilgrim's Progress* also included original, engraved illustrations. As was the case more than three hundred years ago, these new illustrations—beautifully rendered in exquisite detail and faithfulness to the story—will delight a new generation of children and adults and will powerfully reinforce the timeless truths of Bunyan's original story.

It is with much appreciation, then—first to Bunyan for his timeless allegory of eternal realities and then to all those who have had a part in carrying forward the extraordinary Bunyan legacy—that we, as the publisher, commend this new edition of *The Pilgrim's Progress*, for the eternal benefit of all who read this work and for the glory of God alone.

Lane T. Dennis, Ph.D.
President and Publisher, Crossway

Editor's Introduction

by C. J. Lovik

The writings of John Bunyan have been an immeasurable gift to generations of English-speaking Christians. His most famous work, *Pilgrim's Progress*, has provided rich nutrients to the soil out of which practical Christianity has flourished and borne much fruit. Bunyan was the supreme Bible teacher for "everyman." To use an old illustration, it was Bunyan who placed the grain down on the barn floor where the little lambs could reach it, feast, and thrive.

There was nothing elitist or sophisticated about Bunyan, but there was something uniquely profound. Bunyan understood and expounded the timeless eternal truths of Holy Scripture—the miracle of redemptive grace and the battle every pilgrim must wage before he arrives at the Celestial City. And he did it in a way that even the simplest child could understand.

Since the age of nine years old, my appreciation and love for the works of Bunyan, especially *Pilgrim's Progress*, has grown and deepened. There was a time when I rarely heard a sermon in which some incident from *Pilgrim's Progress* was not used to illustrate a biblical truth. Many of those illustrations have guided me through my own pilgrimage. But, sadly, what was such a great benefit to me is enjoyed by only a relative few today.

In my late twenties I began teaching a class called "Pictures from *Pilgrim's Progress*," a title borrowed from Charles Spurgeon. In those days, three or four decades ago, I did not need to ask for a show of hands from those who had read *Pilgrim's Progress*, as all were familiar with the book. Even the unchurched were familiar with *Pilgrim's Progress*, as it was on the required reading list for every public high school student. Today things are much different, and you would be hard-pressed to find one in twenty Christians who have read *Pilgrim's Progress*. For those who are under thirty, the ratio would be even higher. And among those who were familiar with the book, it would typically not be the original text they had read but a children's paraphrase.

Many skilled authors have attempted to bring *Pilgrim's Progress* to modern English readers. I applaud their efforts and respect the desire to reclaim the lost readership this book once enjoyed. But it occurred to me, after reading many of these attempts, that something very important had been lost in the translation. In short, many of the truths that Bunyan so skillfully and artfully proposed had been dulled or skipped over in an attempt to keep the modern reader's interest. In addition much of the antiquity of the work had been lost, and with it was lost the voice and tenor of Bunyan himself.

For anyone who wishes to "update" the original text of *Pilgrim's Progress*, the challenge is indeed great. The English language has changed significantly in the last three hundred and fifty years. Scores of metaphors and sayings that were in common use and understood by all in the seventeenth century are now antiquated or obscure, creating a major obstacle for the modern reader. But in addition to this, the modern English reader often considers Bunyan's literary form of allegory to be antiquated and inconsequential, thereby missing the vibrant truths that are so richly illustrated in Bunyan's allegory.

The challenge of updating Bunyan's classic—in a way that preserves the author's voice and respects the antiquity of the work—was daunting and arduous. For nearly a year this was my constant focus—to prayerfully and carefully discern which stones on the path to leave untouched and which stones to adjust, however slight an adjustment may be necessary, to make the path passable once more (and glorious!) for the modern English reader. Likewise, my goal throughout has always been to respect the literary style of Bunyan and the truths he unfolded in his timeless narrative. The greatest compliment that I could receive after reading this updated edition of *Pilgrim's Progress* is that the reader would be able to honestly say that he has really read and encountered Bunyan and his classic work.

It is my hope and prayer that *Pilgrim's Progress* might once more be a blessing and inspiration to a new generation. Clearly Christians today are in great need of understanding, guidance, and encouragement. Thus it is my dream that in the pulpits of the English-speaking world *Pilgrim's Progress* might once again come into prominence and popular understanding—and likewise in the hearts of individuals and the homes of families around the world. What a tremendous thing it would be if a whole generation were to rediscover the deep, eternal truths of Bunyan's allegory—as an alternative and antidote to the lurid diet of Vanity Fair that is everywhere today in movies, videos, literature, and the Internet.

I have dedicated my efforts on this work to my gracious Lord and Savior, who is the author of all that is good and true. And having said this, I feel an obligation to add one more thing: As wonderful as *Pilgrim's Progress* is, it is not the Bible, nor is it equal to the Bible in any way except as a brilliant commentary on the only Scriptures—the Old and New Testaments. Bunyan wanted his readers to understand that fact; and so, in his absence, I am compelled to pass this along to you—the Scriptures stand alone!

Finally, one cannot read much of Bunyan without coming into contact with his poems and rhymes. When Bunyan's character Christian lost his burden at the foot of the cross, Bunyan exuberantly voiced the unimaginable joy of the event in a poem. This has inspired me to do the same. And so I offer my own poem to you,

Evangelist points Christian to the sheep gate.

Then Evangelist asked, "Why are you not willing to die, since this life is attended with so many evils?"

The man answered, "Because I am afraid that this burden that is on my back will sink me lower than the grave, and I shall fall into Hell.[g]

"And, sir," continued the man, "if I am not ready to die, then I am not prepared to go to judgment and from there to execution. Thinking about these things distresses me greatly."

Then Evangelist said, "If this is your condition, why are you standing still?"

The man responded, "Because I do not know where to go."

Then Evangelist gave him a parchment and unrolled it so that the man could read, "Flee from the wrath to come."[h9]

When he had read it, the man looked at Evangelist very carefully and said, "Which way should I run?"[10]

Then Evangelist, pointing with his finger to a very wide field asked, "Do you see the distant narrow gate?"[i11]

"No," the man replied.

Then Evangelist asked, "Do you see the distant shining light?"[j]

"I think I do," the man answered.

Then Evangelist said, "Keep that light in your eye, and go up directly toward it, and soon you will see the narrow gate. And when you finally come to the gate, knock and you will be told what to do."[12]

So I saw in my dream that the man began to run. He had not run very far from his home when his wife and children, realizing what was happening, cried after him to return.[k] But the man put his fingers in his ears and ran on crying, "Life! Life! Eternal life!" So without looking back, he fled toward the middle of the valley.

The neighbors also came out to see what was going on, and when they saw who it was that was running, some mocked him, others

---

[g]Isaiah 30:33.
[h]Matthew 3:7.
[i]Matthew 7:13–14.
[j]Psalm 119:105; 2 Peter 1:19.
[k]Luke 14:26.

yelled out threats, and some cried after the man to return. Among those were two who decided to bring him back by force. The name of the one was Obstinate, and the name of the other was Pliable.[13]

Now by this time the man was a good distance away. But Obstinate and Pliable were determined to pursue him, which they did. Soon they caught up with him, and he asked them, "Why have you run after me?" The neighbors answered, "To persuade you to go back with us."

"But that is not possible," the man replied. "You live in the City of Destruction, the place where I was born; and I believe that if you stay in that city you will die sooner or later, and then you will sink lower than the grave, into a place that burns with fire and brimstone. Please consider, good neighbors, coming along with me."

"What!" said Obstinate. "And leave our friends and comforts behind us?"

"Yes," said the fleeing man Christian (for that was his name), "because all that you leave behind is not worthy to be compared with even a little of what I am seeking to enjoy.[l] And if you will come along with me and not give up, we will both be blessed with treasure to spare, beyond anything we can imagine.[m] Come along with me and see if what I am telling you is not true."

"What are you looking for?" Obstinate replied. "What is so valuable that you would turn your back on all the world to find it?"

"I am looking," Christian explained, "for an 'inheritance that is imperishable, undefiled, and unfading, kept in Heaven.'[n] It is kept safe there to be given at the appointed time to those who diligently seek it.[o] You can read about it in my book."

"Nonsense!" said Obstinate. "Away with your book. Will you come back with us or not?"

"No!" said Christian. "I have laid my hand to the plow and cannot look back. I have started this journey, and I must finish it."[p]

---

[l] 2 Corinthians 4:18.
[m] Luke 15:17.
[n] 1 Peter 1:4.
[o] Hebrews 11:16.
[p] Luke 9:62.

"Come on, Pliable," Obstinate urged his companion. "Let's turn around and go home without him. There is a group of these mixed-up lunatics who get a crazy idea in their head and are wiser in their own eyes than seven men who can render a reason."[q]

Then Pliable said, "Don't be so harsh. If what the good Christian says is true, the things he is looking for are better than anything we have. I feel like I should go along with my neighbor."

"What! More fools still?" Obstinate replied. "Do what I say, and go back. Who knows where this lunatic will lead you? Go back; go back and be wise."

"Don't listen to him," Christian urged. "Come with me, Pliable. There are things to be gained such as I was telling you about, and many more glories besides. If you don't believe me, read about it in this book; and as far as the trustworthiness of this book goes, it is all confirmed by the blood of Him who made it."[r]

"Well, neighbor Obstinate," said Pliable, "I have come to a decision. I have decided to go along with Christian and to cast in my lot with him." Pliable thought for a second and then turned to Christian and asked, "But do you know the way to the desired place?"

"I was given directions by a man whose name is Evangelist," Christian said. "He told me to go as quickly as I could to the little gate that is just up ahead, and once there we will receive instructions about the way before us."

"Come then, good neighbor," Pliable replied. "Let's be going." Then they went on together.

"And I will go back to my home," said Obstinate. "I will not be a companion of such misled fanatical fellows."

Now I saw in my dream, after Obstinate returned to the City of Destruction, that Christian and Pliable began to talk as they walked together through the middle of the valley. Thus they began to converse.

"I am glad," Christian said, "that you were persuaded to come

[q]Proverbs 26:16.
[r]Hebrews 13:20–21; also Hebrews 9:17–21.

have been trying to repair it for sixteen hundred years. To the best of my knowledge, this place has swallowed up twenty thousand wheelbarrows of wholesome instruction brought from all corners of the King's dominion. But even after all the best material for mending this swamp has been applied, it still remains the Swamp of Despond. There are, by the direction of the Lawgiver, good solid steps placed through the middle of the swamp, but the poor weather and filth that spews from the swamp make them hard to see. Even when the weather is good and the steps plainly seen, some men are so confused and mixed-up that they miss the steps and end up in the swamp. One thing you can be sure of, though—once you go through the narrow gate, the ground is good."[ac]

[ac]2 Samuel 7:23.

Chapter Two

THE WAY OF THE WORLD
OR THE NARROW WAY

ow I saw in my dream that by this time Pliable had returned to his home. Upon his arrival his neighbors came to visit him. Some of his neighbors called him a wise man for coming back. Some called him a fool for starting such a hazardous journey with Christian in the first place. Others mocked Pliable for his cowardliness, saying, "If we had begun such a journey, we would not have abandoned it because of a few difficulties." Embarrassed and pouting, Pliable hid himself for a time. But at last he got a little of his confidence back and joined in with the others in deriding poor Christian behind his back.

Now as Christian was walking by himself, he spied someone far-off, crossing over the field to meet him. When their paths crossed, the gentleman who met up with Christian introduced himself as Mr. Worldly-Wiseman. He lived in the town of Carnal Policy, a very great town that was near the place from which Christian had come.[1]

Mr. Worldly-Wiseman immediately suspected that Christian was the person who had set out from the City of Destruction, since news of his departure had spread as far as the cities and towns surrounding Christian's former home. As Mr. Worldly-Wiseman viewed Christian's disheveled appearance and heard his sighs and groans, he was convinced that this was the rumored man and began to talk to him.[2]

"Where are you going?" Mr. Worldly-Wiseman asked. "How did you get yourself into such bad shape, and what are you doing with this great burden on your back?"

"Indeed," Christian replied, "a burden heavy as any creature ever had! And since you ask me, 'Where are you going?' I will tell you, sir. I am going to the small sheep gate that lies ahead, for I am informed that there will I enter into a way where I will soon get rid of my heavy burden."

"Do you have a wife and children?" Worldly-Wiseman asked.

"Yes, but I am so oppressed by this burden that I cannot take pleasure in my family as I used to. I now feel as if I am a man who has no family."[a]

"Will you listen to me if I give you counsel?"

"If it is good I will, for I stand in need of good counsel," Christian replied.

"I advise you to quickly get rid of your burden," Worldly-Wiseman explained, "for you will never be settled in your mind until then, nor will you enjoy the benefits of the blessings that God has given you."[3]

"That is what I am seeking," said Christian. "I want nothing more than to be rid of this heavy burden. But I cannot free myself from it, nor is there any man in our country who can take it off my shoulders. That is why I am going toward the small gate ahead, as I told you, so that I may be rid of my burden."

"Who told you to go this way to be rid of your burden?"

Christian answered, "He was a man who appeared to be very honorable and great. His name, as I recall, was Evangelist."

"Shame on him for such counsel!" Worldly-Wiseman protested. "There is not a more dangerous and troublesome way in the world

---

[a]1 Corinthians 7:29.

than the way he has directed you. Look at the difficulty you have experienced already. I can see that you are already covered in dirt from the Swamp of Despond. Listen to me: that swamp is only the beginning of the sorrows and troubles you will find if you follow that way. Hear what I have to say since I am older than you: if you continue on the way that Evangelist has directed, your journey will be attended by weariness, pain, hunger, perils, nakedness, sword, lions, dragons, darkness, and, in a word, death! The truth of what I am telling you has been confirmed by many testimonies. Why should a man so carelessly cast himself into such peril by giving heed to a stranger?"

"Why, sir," Christian said, "this burden upon my back is more terrible to me than all the things that you have mentioned. I do not care what I meet with on the way, as long as I can also meet with deliverance from my burden."

"How did you come to bear this burden in the first place?" Worldly-Wiseman asked.

"By reading this book in my hand."

"I thought so," Worldly-Wiseman stated softly. "What has happened to you has also happened to other weak men who meddle with things too high for them. You see," said the old gentleman, "you have suddenly been distracted from the important things that matter most to men. You have lost your proper focus on life, and the distractions that now command your attention will cause you to do desperate things in order to obtain something you do not even understand."[4]

"I know that I wish to obtain ease from my heavy burden."

Worldly-Wiseman went on, "But why do you seek ease from your burden in a way that is surrounded by so many dangers? If you only had the patience to hear me, I could direct you to a place where you could obtain your desire without the dangers you are now headed for. Listen to me, and I will show you a safe remedy. Furthermore, be assured that instead of those dangers, you will meet with much safety, friendship, and contentment."[5]

Mr. Worldly-Wiseman directs Christian out of the way.

Then Christian fell down at Evangelist's feet as if he were dead, crying, "Woe is me, for I am undone!"

When Evangelist saw this, he lifted him up with his right hand and said, "Every sin and blasphemy will be forgiven people.[f] Do not disbelieve, but believe."[g] Christian regained some of his strength and stood up trembling before Evangelist.

Then Evangelist proceeded, saying, "Give earnest attention to the things that I am going to tell you. I will now show you who it was that deluded you and to whom it was that he sent you.

"The man that met you is named Mr. Worldly-Wiseman, and he is well named because he loves only the doctrine of this world[h] (he always goes to the town of Morality to attend church). He loves that doctrine best because it keeps him away from the cross.[i] And because he is of this fleshly disposition, he tries to direct poor sinners away from the path to which I send them, even though it is the only right path. Now there are three things in this man's counsel that you must utterly abhor:

"1. His convincing you to leave the right path.

"2. His effort to make the cross repulsive to you.

"3. His sending you on a way that leads to death.

"First, you must abhor his turning you out of the right way and also your own willingness to consent to his counsel. You must hate it because this is to reject the counsel of God in exchange for the counsel of a Worldly-Wiseman. The Lord says, 'Strive to enter in through the narrow door,[j] the narrow door to which I send you; for the gate is narrow and the way is hard that leads to life, and those who find it are few.'[k]

"From this narrow gate, and from the way that leads to it, has this wicked man turned you, and by so doing he has almost brought you to your own destruction. You must hate that he

---

[f] Matthew 12:31; Mark 3:28.
[g] John 20:27.
[h] 1 John 4:5.
[i] Galatians 6:12.
[j] Luke 13:24.
[k] Matthew 7:14.

turned you out of the right way and abhor yourself for listening to him.

"Secondly, you must abhor his effort to make the cross loath-some to you, for the cross is what you are to prefer above all else, even more than all the treasures of Egypt.[l] Besides, the King of glory has told you that 'whoever finds his life will lose it.'[m] And, 'If anyone comes to me and does not hate his own father and mother and wife and children and brothers and sisters, yes, and even his own life, he cannot be my disciple.'[n] Anyone who tries to persuade you otherwise is opposing the only truth by which you can have eternal life. And you must hate all such doctrines.

"Thirdly, you must hate that he directed you into a way that leads to death. You must also know about the person to whom he sent you, and how unable that person is to deliver you from your burden.

"The person to whom you were sent for relief, whose name is Legality, is the son of the slave woman who, with all her children, is still in bondage. The mountain that you feared would fall on your head is Mount Sinai. Now if the slave woman and all her children are in bondage, how can you expect them to set you free from your burden?

"This Mr. Legality is not able to loose you of your burden. No man has ever gotten rid of his burden by Mr. Legality's help, nor are any going to. You cannot be set free by the works of the Law, for by the deeds of the Law no man living is able to get rid of his burden.

"Mr. Worldly-Wiseman is an alien, and Mr. Legality is a cheat. As for his son Civility, notwithstanding his pleasant looks, he is nothing more than a hypocrite who is also unable to help you. Believe me, there is nothing in all the noise that you heard from these dull men but an intent to rob you of your salvation by turning you away from the way in which I directed you."

After this, Evangelist called aloud to the heavens for confirma-

---

[l]Hebrews 11:25–26.
[m]Mark 8:35; John 12:25; Matthew 10:39.
[n]Luke 14:26.

tion of what he had said, and with that there came words and fire out of the mountain under which poor Christian stood that made his hair stand on end. The words that Christian heard were these: "For all who rely on works of the law are 'under a curse': for it is written, 'Cursed be everyone who does not abide by all things written in the Book of the Law, and do them.'"[o]

Now Christian looked for nothing but death and began to cry out desperately, even cursing the time that he had met with Mr. Worldly-Wiseman, calling himself a thousand fools for listening to his counsel. He also was greatly ashamed to think that this gentleman's arguments, flowing only from the deception of the flesh, should have persuaded him to forsake the right way. After this, he approached Evangelist with the following words and thoughts.

Christian asked, "Sir, what do you think? Is there hope for me? May I go back to the way and up to the sheep gate? Will I be abandoned for this and sent back from where I came, disgraced and ashamed? I am sorry I listened to Worldly-Wiseman's counsel. Can my sins be forgiven?"

Then Evangelist said to him, "Your sin is very great, for by it you have committed two evils: you have forsaken the way that is good, and you have walked in forbidden paths. Yet will the man at the gate receive you, for he has goodwill for men."

Then Evangelist warned Christian to be careful and not to turn aside again, "lest you perish in the way, for His wrath is quickly kindled."[p]

Then Christian asked to go back to the way leading to the narrow sheep gate, and Evangelist, after he had kissed him, gave him a smile and bid him Godspeed.

So Christian went on with haste. He spoke to no one as he quickly returned to the path that led to the small sheep gate, and if anyone asked him a question, Christian would not even give him an answer.

---

[o]Galatians 3:10.
[p]Psalm 2:12.

Christian knocks on the sheep gate.

"The man in this picture represents one of a thousand: he can conceive children,[t] travail in birth with children,[u] and nurse them himself when they are born. You see him with his eyes lifted up to Heaven, the best of books in his hand and the law of truth written on his lips. All this is to show you that his work is to know and unfold dark things to sinners. You see him pleading with men, the world cast behind him, and a crown hanging over his head to show you that by rejecting and despising the things of this present world for the love that he has for his Master's service, he is sure to have glory as his reward in the world to come. I have shown you this picture first because the man whom it represents is the only man authorized by the Lord of the place where you are going to be your guide in all the difficult places you will encounter on the way. So pay attention to what I have shown you, and keep this picture foremost in your mind, so that if you meet with someone who doesn't resemble this picture's likeness but who pretends to lead you in the right way, you will not follow him down to destruction."

Then the Interpreter took Christian by the hand and led him into a very large parlor that was full of dust because it was never swept. After He had reviewed it a little while, the Interpreter called for a man to come and sweep. Now when he began to sweep, the dust began to fly about so much and was so thick that Christian almost choked. Then said the Interpreter to a damsel who stood nearby, "Bring water, and sprinkle the room." When she had done as requested, it was swept and cleansed very pleasantly.

Then Christian asked, "What does this mean?"

The Interpreter answered, "This parlor is the heart of a man that has never been sanctified by the sweet grace of the gospel; the dust is his original sin and inward corruptions that have defiled the whole man. The first man that began to sweep is the Law; the damsel that brought water and sprinkled it is the gospel. You saw that as soon as the first man began to sweep, the dust filled the room

---

[t]1 Corinthians 4:15.
[u]Galatians 4:19.

so thickly that it could not be cleansed, and you almost choked on it. This is to show you that the Law, instead of cleansing the heart from sin, actually revives, increases, and adds strength to it. Even though the Law uncovers and forbids sin, it is powerless to conquer or subdue it at all.[v]

"Then you saw the damsel sprinkle the room with water, after which it was pleasingly cleansed. This is to show you the way in which the gospel comes into the heart with its sweet and precious influences. You saw the damsel clear the dust from the room by sprinkling the floor with water. This shows how sin is vanquished and subdued and the soul made clean through faith and consequently fit for the King of glory to inhabit."[w]

I also saw in my dream that the Interpreter took Christian by the hand into a little room where there sat two little children, each one in his own chair. The name of the older child was Passion, and the name of the younger was Patience. Passion seemed to be very discontent, but Patience was very quiet. Then Christian asked, "What is the reason for the discontentment of Passion?"

The Interpreter answered, "Their Guardian would have them wait for their best things until the beginning of next year. Passion wants it all now, but Patience is willing to wait."

Then I saw that someone came to Passion and brought him a bag of treasure, pouring it at his feet. Passion picked up the treasure rejoicing and laughed Patience to scorn. But as I watched for a while, all the treasure either rusted or molded away, and soon he had nothing left but rust and rags.

Then Christian asked the Interpreter to explain this more fully to him.

So he said, "These two lads are figures: Passion, of the men of this world, and Patience, of the men of that world which is to come. You saw that Passion wanted to have it all now, this year. In other words, the men of this world want all their good things now, in this

---

[v]Romans 7:6; 1 Corinthians 15:56; Romans 5:20.
[w]John 15:3; Ephesians 5:26; Acts 15:9; Romans 16:25–26; John 15:13.

open before him. He was writing the names of those who wished to enter the palace. Christian also saw in the doorway many armed men who were determined to inflict as many injuries and wounds as they could on anyone trying to enter the palace.

Christian was amazed. At last, after every man retreated back for fear of the armed men, Christian saw a man with a very determined look on his face come up to the man sitting at the table and say, "Set down my name, sir." As soon as his name was written in the book, Christian saw the man draw his sword, put a helmet upon his head, and rush toward the armed men at the door, who tried to stop him with deadly force. But the man, not at all discouraged, began cutting and hacking most fiercely at his attackers.

After he had received and given many wounds to those who attempted to keep him out, he cut his way through them all[aa] and pressed forward into the palace. Then Christian heard a pleasant voice from those who were inside the palace, even those who walked upon the top of the palace, saying, "Come in, come in; eternal glory you shall win."

So the determined man went in and was clothed with gold. Then Christian smiled and said, "I think I know what this means, and I think it is time for me to continue my journey."

"No," said the Interpreter. "Stay until I have shown you a little more, and after that you can go on your way." So he took Christian by the hand and led him into a very dark room, where a man sat in an iron cage.

The man in the cage seemed very sad. He sat with his eyes looking down to the ground, his hands folded together, and he sighed as if his heart would break. Then Christian asked, "What does this mean?" Instead of answering, the Interpreter asked Christian to talk with the man.

So Christian asked the man, "Who are you?"

The man answered, "I am not who I used to be."

"Who did you used to be?" Christian asked.

[aa]Acts 14:22.

The man said, "I was once fair and flourishing in my profession of faith, both in my own eyes and also in the eyes of others. I was, I once thought, deserving of the Celestial City and was full of joy as I considered going there."[ab]

Christian inquired, "Well, who are you now?"

The man replied, "I am now a man of despair, and it surrounds me as does this iron cage. I cannot get out. O now I cannot!"

"But how did you come to be in this condition?" Christian asked him.

He answered honestly, "I stopped being watchful and diligent. I rushed after my own lusts. I sinned against the light of the Word and the goodness of God. I have grieved the Spirit, and He is gone. I tempted the Devil, and he has come to me. I have provoked God to anger, and He has left me. I have so hardened my heart that I cannot repent."

Then Christian asked the Interpreter, "Is there no hope for such a man as this?"

"Ask him," said the Interpreter.

So Christian asked the man, "Is there no hope? Must you be kept in the iron cage of despair?"

"No hope, none at all," replied the man in the iron cage.

"But consider this: the Son of the Blessed is full of pity."

The man protested, "I have crucified Him to myself afresh;[ac] I have despised His person;[ad] I have despised His righteousness; I have 'counted His blood an unholy thing'; I have 'insulted the Spirit of grace.'[ae] Therefore, I have shut myself out of all the promises, and there now remains to me nothing but threatenings, dreadful threatenings, fearful threatenings of certain judgment and fiery indignation, which shall devour me as an adversary."

"How did you bring yourself into this condition?"

The man explained, "I promised myself much delight from the

[ab]Luke 8:13.
[ac]Hebrews 6:6.
[ad]Luke 19:14.
[ae]Hebrews 10:28–29.

lusts, pleasures, and the profits of this world. But now every one of those things wounds me and gnaws at me like a burning worm."

"But can't you even now repent and turn away from those things?" Christian asked hopefully.

"God has denied me repentance," the man said. "His Word gives me no encouragement to believe. He Himself has shut me up in this iron cage, and all the men in the world do not have the power to let me out. O eternity! Eternity! How will I deal with the misery that waits for me in eternity!"

Then the Interpreter said to Christian, "Remember this man's misery, and let it be an everlasting caution to you."

"Well," Christian said, "this is fearful! May God help me to watch and be sober and pray, that I may avoid the cause of this man's misery! But, sir, isn't it time for me to go on my way?"

Interpreter added, "Stay until I show you one more thing, and then you may go on your way."

So he took Christian by the hand again and led him into a chamber, where there was a man getting out of bed; and as he dressed himself, he shook and trembled. Then Christian asked, "Why does this man tremble?"

The Interpreter then called the man over and told him to tell Christian the reason for his trembling. This is what the man told Christian:

"This night, as I was in my sleep, I dreamed and witnessed the heavens grow pitch-black. I also heard and saw the most terrible thunder and lightning; so I looked up in my dream and saw the clouds begin to roll in at an unusual rate of speed. Then I heard the great sound of a trumpet and saw a Man sitting upon a great cloud, attended by thousands from Heaven. They were all clothed in flaming fire, and the heavens were as a burning flame. I then heard a voice saying, 'Arise, you that are dead, and come to judgment.' With that the rocks split, the graves opened, and the dead who were in them came out. Some of them were extremely glad and looked upward, and some tried to hide themselves under the mountains for fear.[af] Then I saw the Man who sat upon the cloud open a book and bid the world come near. A fierce flame spewed out from before Him, creating a barrier between Him and the world of men, like the barrier between a judge and the prisoners at the bar.[ag]

"I heard the Man who sat on the cloud proclaim to the heavenly hosts who attended Him, 'Gather together the tares, the chaff, and stubble, and cast them into the burning lake.'[ah] And immediately the bottomless pit opened, just where I stood. And out of the mouth of that pit came smoke and the coals of fire, accompanied by hideous noises. Then I heard the Man who sat on the clouds proclaim to the heavenly host, 'Gather My wheat into my barn.'[ai] And with that I saw many people caught up and carried away into the clouds, but I was left behind.[aj] I tried to hide myself, but I could not, for the Man who sat upon the cloud kept his eye upon me; my sins also came into my mind, and my conscience accused me without mercy.[ak] Then I woke from my sleep."

Christian asked, "But what was it that made you so afraid of this sight?"

He explained, "Why, I thought that the Day of Judgment was come and that I was not ready for it. But what frightened me most was that the angels gathered up others but left me behind. Also the pit of Hell opened her mouth just below where I stood. My conscience also afflicted me, and I thought the Judge had His eye upon me, and I saw in His expression both anger and indignation."

Then said the Interpreter to Christian, "Have you considered all these things?"

"Yes," Christian answered, "and they cause me to both hope and fear."

Interpreter told him seriously, "Keep all these things in your mind as a constant encouragement and warning as you journey on

---

[af]1 Corinthians 15:52; 1 Thessalonians 4:16; Jude 14; John 5:28–29; 2 Thessalonians 1:7–8; Revelation 20:11–14; Isaiah 26:21; Micah 7:16–17; Psalm 95:1–3; Daniel 10:7.
[ag]Malachi 3:2–3; Daniel 7:9–10.
[ah]Matthew 3:12; 13:30; Malachi 4:1.
[ai]Luke 3:17.
[aj]1 Thessalonians 4:16–17.
[ak]Romans 2:14–15.

ahead to the Celestial City." Then Christian began to prepare himself for the journey ahead, and when he was ready to depart, the Interpreter said, "May the Comforter be with you always to guide you in the way that leads to the City."

So Christian went on his way, saying, "Here I have seen things rare and profitable, things pleasant and dreadful, things to give me stability and wisdom to deal with my tasks at hand. For showing me what I need to understand for the journey ahead, I thank You, good Interpreter."

Christian's burden comes loose at the cross.

Chapter Three

A Burden Lifted and a Journey Begun

Now I saw in my dream that the highway up which Christian was to go was fenced on each side with a wall; the wall was called Salvation.[a] Therefore, it was up this highway that Christian ran, but not without great difficulty because of the burden of the load on his back.[1]

He ran till he came to a small hill, at the top of which stood a cross and at the bottom of which was a tomb. I saw in my dream that when Christian walked up the hill to the cross, his burden came loose from his shoulders and fell off his back, tumbling down the hill until it came to the mouth of the tomb, where it fell in to be seen no more.

Then Christian was relieved and delighted and exclaimed with a joyful heart, "He has given me rest by His sorrow and life by His death." For a while he stood still in front of the cross to look and wonder; it was very surprising to him that the sight of the cross should ease him of his burden. He continued looking at the cross until tears began streaming down his cheeks.[b][2] As he stood looking and weeping,

---

[a]Isaiah 26:1.
[b]Zechariah 12:10.

three Shining Ones came to him and greeted him with, "Peace be with you." Then the first said to him, "Your sins are forgiven."[c] The second stripped him of his rags and dressed him with new clothing.[d] The third put a mark on his forehead and gave him a scroll with a seal on it. He told Christian to review it often as he went on his way and at the end of his journey to turn it in at the Celestial Gate.[e][3] After this they went their way.

Then Christian gave three leaps for joy and went on his way singing:

"Thus far I did come,
Burdened with my sin.
Nor could I find relief
From my grief within.

Until here I came,
What a place this is!
Here shall be the beginning,
Of full, eternal bliss!

Now my burden falls
From my back forever.
From the cords that bound it,
By grace my grief is severed.

Blessed cross! Blessed tomb!
Rather, most blessed be
The Man who there was put to shame,
A shame He took for me!"

I saw then in my dream that Christian went on until he came to the bottom of the hill. There he saw lying by the side of the path three men fast asleep, with chains upon their feet. The name of the one was Foolish, the second Sloth, and the third Presumption.[4]

Christian went to them to see if he might awaken them and said to them, "'You will be like one who lies down in the midst of the sea,

[c]Mark 2:5.
[d]Zechariah 3:4.
[e]Ephesians 1:13.

Formalist and Hypocrisy trespass over the Wall of Salvation.

like one who lies on top of a mast,'[f] though the Dead Sea is under you, a gulf that has no bottom. Wake up and get back on the path, and if you are willing, I will help you take off your iron shackles." He also told them, "If he that 'goes about like a roaring lion' comes by and finds you like this, he will destroy you with his teeth."[g] With that they looked at Christian and began to reply to him. Foolish said, "I see no danger." Sloth said, "I just need a little more sleep." And Presumption said, "Everyone needs to make his own choices. You need to mind your own business and not meddle in ours." So they all lay down to sleep again, and Christian went on his way.

Christian was troubled to think that men in such danger should have so little regard for the kindness he had extended when he awakened them, counseled them, and offered to free them of their iron shackles.[5] As he was thinking about this, he saw two men come tumbling over the wall on the left side and onto the path. They immediately came toward Christian. The name of the one was Formalist, and the name of the other was Hypocrisy. Soon they were walking with Christian on the path. Christian immediately began to engage them in conversation.[6]

Christian asked, "Gentlemen, where did you come from, and where are you going?"

Formality and Hypocrisy replied, "We were born in the land of Vain-Glory and are going to Mount Zion where we expect we will receive both praise and honor."

"Why didn't you enter by the gate that stands at the beginning of the way? Don't you know that it is written that 'he who does not come in by the door but climbs up some other way is a thief and a robber'?"[h]

Formalist and Hypocrisy answered that to go to the gate in order to enter into the way was considered by them and all their countrymen to be too inconvenient and roundabout, especially since

[f]Proverbs 23:34.
[g]1 Peter 5:8.
[h]John 10:1.

they could shorten the journey by simply climbing over the wall, as they had done.

"But won't this be seen as trespassing?" Christian asked. "Don't you think the Lord of the City for which we are bound must count it as a violation of His revealed will?"

Formalist and Hypocrisy told Christian not to worry about it since it had been the custom of their land for more than a thousand years.

"But," asked Christian, "will your custom stand up in a court of law?"

They replied, "This custom of entering the way by taking a shortcut has been going on as a long-standing practice for more than a thousand years and would be ruled as a legal practice by any impartial judge. And besides," they added, "as long as we get into the way, what does it matter how we get in? If we are in, we are in. You came into the way through the narrow gate, and we came tumbling over the wall, and since we are both in, who is to say that your chosen path is better than ours?"

Christian told them, "I walk by the rule of my Master; you walk by the rude working of your own notions. You are condemned as thieves already by the Lord of the way; therefore, I doubt you will be found as true men at the end of the journey. You came in by yourselves, without His direction, and will go out by yourselves, without His mercy."

To this they had little to say, except to tell Christian to mind his own business. Then I saw that Formalist and Hypocrisy went along with Christian, saying only that as far as the laws and ordinances were concerned, they would obey them as conscientiously as Christian. They added that they saw no difference between themselves and Christian except for the coat he wore, which they speculated was given to Christian to hide his shame and nakedness.

Christian responded, "You will not be saved by keeping laws and ordinances. You cannot be saved, because you did not come in

Christian begins his journey up the Hill Difficulty.

by the door.[i] As for the coat that is on my back, it was given to me by the Lord of the place where I am going and is, as you say, a cover for my nakedness. I take it as a token of His kindness to me, for I had nothing but rags before. Besides, I take some comfort in the fact that when I come to the gate of the City, the Lord of that place will surely recognize me since it is His coat on my back, a coat that He gave me the day that He stripped me of my rags.

"I also have a mark on my forehead, which perhaps you have not noticed. One of my Lord's most intimate associates placed it on my forehead the day that my burden fell off my shoulders.

"Also I have been given a scroll to read as a comfort to me as I make my journey. I was also told to turn it in at the Celestial Gate as an assurance that I will be welcomed into the Celestial City. I doubt you have any interest in all these things since you did not come in at the gate."

To this, Formalist and Hypocrisy gave no reply. They just looked at each other and laughed.

Then I saw that they all kept walking along the path, except that Christian walked up ahead and had no more conversation with Formalist and Hypocrisy. He only talked with himself, sometimes sighing, sometimes encouraging himself, and often refreshing himself by reading from the scroll that one of the Shining Ones had given him.

I saw, then, that they all went on until they came to the foot of the Hill Difficulty,[7] at the bottom of which was a spring of fresh water. Here the men were faced with a choice of three paths. The path that led directly from the gate continued straight up the steep hill. Another path turned to the left and a third to the right of the hill. Christian went to the spring and drank until he was no longer thirsty[j] and then began to go up the Hill Difficulty, saying:

> *"The hill, though high, I desire to ascend,*
> *The difficulty will not me offend;*

---

[i] Galatians 2:16.
[j] Isaiah 49:10.

For I perceive the way to life lies here.
Be strong, my heart, let's neither faint nor fear;
Better, though difficult, the right way to go,
Than wrong, though easy, where the end is woe."

Formalist and Hypocrisy also came to the foot of the hill, but when they saw how steep and high it was and that there were two simpler ways to go, they chose the ways that looked easier. They supposed that the two ways would go around the hill and meet up again with the straight way that Christian was taking. Now the name of one of those ways was Danger, and the name of the other was Destruction. So Formalist took the way that is called Danger, which led him into a great wooded area; and Hypocrisy went the way to Destruction, which led him into a wide field full of dark mountains, where he stumbled, fell, and never got up.

I looked and saw Christian go up the hill, where I noticed him slowing his pace from running to walking and finally to scrambling up the path on his hands and knees because it was very steep.

Now I saw that about halfway up the hill there was a pleasant arbor built by the Lord of the hill for the refreshment of weary travelers. When Christian reached this spot, he sat down to rest.

Then he pulled his scroll out from under his coat and was comforted by what he read. He also took a fresh look at the coat that had been given to him earlier when he stood by the cross. As he entertained pleasant thoughts about the changes that had taken place in his life, he at last fell into a slumber and finally into a deep sleep, from which he did not awake until it was almost night; and in his sleep, his scroll fell out of his hand.[8]

Now, as he was sleeping, someone came to him and awakened him, saying, "Go to the ant, O sluggard; consider her ways and be wise."[k] And with that Christian sprang up and sped on his way. He had not traveled far when he came to the top of the hill.

Now, at the top of the hill, two men came running to meet him. The name of the one was Timorous and of the other Mistrust, to

---

[k]Proverbs 6:6.

Christian sleeps in the arbor on the Hill Difficulty.

whom Christian said, "Sirs, what's the matter? You're running the wrong way."[9]

Timorous answered that they were going to the City of Zion and had climbed up the Hill Difficulty. "But," he added, "the farther we went, the more danger we encountered. So we turned around and are going back from where we came."

"Yes," said Mistrust, "for just ahead there are a couple of lions in the way—we don't know if they are sleeping or awake. But we are sure that if we came within their reach, they would pull us to pieces."

Then Christian said, "You're making me afraid. Where shall I run to be safe? If I go back to my own country, which is prepared for fire and brimstone, I shall certainly perish. If I can get to the Celestial City, I am sure to be safe. I must go forward. To go back is nothing but death; to go forward is fear of death, and life everlasting beyond it. I will go forward."

So Mistrust and Timorous ran down the hill, and Christian went on his way. But thinking again of what he had just heard from the men, he felt in his coat for his scroll so that he might read it and be comforted; but it was not there.

Then Christian was in great distress and didn't know what to do. He wanted to be comforted by the words in the scroll and also knew it was his pass into the Celestial City.

He stood still and became very perplexed and didn't know what to do. At last he remembered that he had slept in the arbor that is on the side of the hill. Falling down upon his knees, he asked God's forgiveness for his foolish act and then went back to look for his scroll.

All the way as he went back, there was a great sorrow in Christian's heart. Sometimes he sighed, sometimes he wept, and oftentimes he chided himself for being so foolish as to fall asleep in that place, which was only erected for a little refreshment for the weary. So he went all the way to the arbor, carefully looking on this side and on that, hoping he might find the scroll that had been such a comfort to him on his journey.

Finally he came within sight of the arbor where he had previously sat and slept. The sight of the place renewed his sorrow as he remembered again how wrong he had been to fall asleep.[1]

He began crying over his sinful sleep, saying, "O wretched man that I am, that I should sleep in the daytime, that I should sleep in the midst of difficulty, that I should so indulge the flesh as to use that rest to ease my flesh, which the Lord of the hill intended only for the relief of the spirits of pilgrims!

"How many steps have I taken in vain! This is what happened to Israel for their sin. They were sent back again by the way of the Red Sea. I am now retracing those steps with sorrow that I might have traveled with delight, had it not been for this sinful sleep. How far I might have been on my way by this time! I am forced to retrace those steps three times over that I should have traveled only once. Now I am about to enter the darkness of night, for the day is almost over. Oh, that I had not slept."[10]

Christian sat down in the arbor and wept, but at last looking sorrowfully down under the seat, he spied his scroll. With trembling and haste he snatched it up and put it into his coat. No one could have been more joyful than this man was after he retrieved his scroll! The scroll was the assurance of his life and acceptance at the Celestial City. He placed it carefully in his coat, gave thanks to God for directing his eyes to the place where it lay, and with joy and tears began his journey again.

Christian nimbly went up the rest of the hill. But before he reached the top of the hill, the sun went down. He recalled again the vanity of sleeping at the arbor; and so he began to talk with himself.

"O sinful sleep; for that little rest I am now making my journey in the dark of night! I must walk without the sun; darkness must cover the path of my feet; and I must hear the noise of the doleful creatures because of my sinful sleep."[m]

Just then he remembered the story that Mistrust and Timorous

---

[1] 1 Thessalonians 5:7–8; Revelation 2:5.
[m] 1 Thessalonians 5:6–7.

Christian is terrified by the lions.

had told him of how they were frightened by the sight of the lions. Then Christian said to himself, "These beasts prowl in the night looking for their prey, and if they should meet with me in the dark, how can I escape from them? How should I keep from being torn in pieces by them?"

With these thoughts in his mind, he went on his way. But while he was fretting over his unhappy circumstances, he lifted up his eyes and beheld a very stately palace in front of him. The name of the place was House Beautiful, and it stood by the side of the highway.[11]

So I saw in my dream that he quickly walked forward, hoping he might find lodging. But before he had gone far, he entered into a very narrow passage, which was about a furlong off the porter's lodge. Looking very carefully ahead as he went, he spied two lions in the way.

"Now," he thought, "I see the dangers that drove Mistrust and Timorous back." The lions were chained, but he did not see the chains. Then he was afraid and thought about going back, seeing nothing but death ahead of him.

Just then the porter at the lodge, whose name is Watchful, seeing that Christian had stopped his progress as if he would go back, cried out to him, asking, "Is your strength so small?[n] Don't fear the lions, for they are chained and are placed there to test your faith and to discover those who have none. Keep in the middle of the path, and no harm shall come to you.

> *"Difficulty is behind, Fear is before.*
> *Though he's got on the hill, the lions roar.*
> *A Christian man is never long at ease.*
> *When one fright's gone, another does him seize."*

Then I saw that Christian went forward, trembling for fear of the lions, but carefully following the directions of the porter.[12] He heard them roar, but they did him no harm. Then he clapped his

---

[n] Mark 8:34–37.

hands and went on until he came and stood in front of the gate where the porter was.

Then said Christian to the porter, "Sir, whose house is this? And may I lodge here tonight?"

The porter answered, "This house was built by the Lord of the hill. He built it for the relief and security of pilgrims." The porter also asked Christian where he was from and where he was going.[13]

"I am come from the City of Destruction and am going to Mount Zion," Christian replied, "but because the sun has now set, I was hoping to lodge here tonight."

The porter inquired, "What is your name?"

"My name is now Christian, but my name used to be Graceless. I came of the race of Japheth, whom God will persuade to dwell in the tents of Shem."°

"But why is it that you come so late?" the porter asked. "The sun has indeed set."

Christian replied, "I would have been here sooner, but 'wretched man that I am!' I slept in the arbor that stands on the hillside, and in my sleep I lost my scroll. I traveled without it to the brow of the hill, where I searched for it but could not find it. I was then forced, with a sorrowful heart, to go back to the arbor where I had slept. It was there I recovered my scroll, and now I am here."

The porter stated, "Well, I will call out one of the virgins of this place who will, if she approves of your testimony, bring you in to the rest of the family, according to the rules of the house."

Then Watchful, the porter, rang a bell, at the sound of which a serious-looking, beautiful maiden came out of the door of the house. Her name was Discretion, and she immediately asked why she had been called.

The porter answered, "This man is on a journey from the City of Destruction to Mount Zion, but being weary and with night coming on he has asked me if he might lodge here tonight. I told him I would call for you, who, after having a conversation with

---

°Genesis 9:27.

Christian is greeted outside the House Beautiful.

him, may do what seems best to you, even according to the law of the house."

Then she asked Christian where he was from and where he was going, and he told her. She asked him also how he got into the way, and he told her. Then she asked him what he had seen and met with in the way, to which he replied, "My name is Christian, and I have a very strong desire to lodge here tonight because from what I perceive, this place was built by the Lord of the hill for the relief and security of pilgrims." So she smiled, with tears in her eyes; and after a short pause, she said, "I will call for two or three more of the family."

So she ran to the door and called out for Prudence, Piety, and Charity, who after a little more conversation with him invited him to meet the family. Many of them met him at the threshold of the house. "Come in," they said, "you are blessed of the Lord. This house was built by the Lord of the hill for the purpose of showing hospitality to pilgrims such as yourself." Then he bowed his head and followed them into the house.

When he had come in and sat down, they gave him something to drink and conversed together until supper was ready. Some of them passed the time profitably with very interesting discussions. Finally they asked Piety and Prudence and Charity to converse with him.

Piety began, "Come, good Christian, since we have received you into our home with such charity this night, let's spend our time profitably by discussing all the things that have happened to you so far on your journey."

Christian responded, "I am glad you are interested in my journey and would be happy to share my adventures with you."

"What was the first thing that motivated you to become a pilgrim?" Piety asked.

"I was driven out of my native country by a dreadful message that I could not get out of my head, and the message was that destruction was unavoidable if I stayed in the place where I was."

Christian is entertained at the House Beautiful.

hindered them was my great concern that I not sin against God or do any wrong to my neighbor."

Charity commented, "Indeed Cain hated his brother 'because his own works were evil, and his brother's righteous.'ᵗ And if your wife and children have been offended with you for this, they show themselves to be implacable to good, and 'you will have delivered your soul' from their blood."ᵘ

Now I saw in my dream that they sat talking together until supper was ready. So when all was prepared and ready, they sat down to eat. Now the table was furnished with savory foods and with wine that was well refined, and all their conversation at the table was about the Lord of the hill.

They spoke with reverence about what He had done and why He did what He did and the reason He built that house. And by the things they said, I perceived that He had been a great warrior. He had fought with and slain "him that had the power of death," but not without great danger to Himself.ᵛ Hearing this made me love Him even more.

They said, and I believe (as said Christian), that He did it with the loss of much blood. But what made it most glorious and gracious was that He did it all out of pure love to His country. And besides, some of the household said they had spoken with Him since He died on the cross; and they have attested that they heard it from His own lips that there is nowhere to be found, no matter how far one might travel, anyone who had a greater love for poor pilgrims than He.

They, moreover, gave an instance of what they heard Him say, which was that He had stripped Himself of His glory that He might do this for the poor. They also heard Him say and affirm "that He would not dwell in the mountain of Zion alone." They said also that He had made many pilgrims into princes, even though by nature they were born beggars, and their original dwelling had been the dunghill.ʷ

ᵗ1 John 3:12.
ᵘEzekiel 3:19.
ᵛHebrews 2:14–15.
ʷ1 Samuel 2:8; Psalm 113:7.

Then he asked the name of the country. They said it was Immanuel's Land; and "like this hill it is for all the pilgrims. And when you go there, with the assistance of the shepherds who live there, you may see the gates of the Celestial City."

Now they all agreed that Christian was ready to go forward on his journey. But they wanted to visit the armory one last time before he left.

So they did, and while they were there, they covered him from head to foot with armor to protect him should he be assaulted along the way. Christian, now dressed in full armor, went with his friends to the gate.[14] When he arrived at the gate, he asked the porter if any other pilgrims had passed by. The porter answered, "Yes."

"Did you ask him his name?" Christian inquired.

The porter replied, "I asked him his name, and he told me it was Faithful."

"Oh," said Christian, "I know him. He is my townsman, a close neighbor. He comes from the place where I was born. How far ahead do you think he is?"

The porter responded, "By this time I think he should be below the hill."

"Well," said Christian, "good porter, the Lord be with you and increase your blessings for all the kindness you have shown me."

Then he began to go forward. Discretion, Piety, Charity, and Prudence accompanied him down to the foot of the hill. And they all went on together, rehearsing their former conversations until they came to the top of the hill.

Then Christian said, "It appears that going down the hill is going to be as difficult and dangerous as it was climbing up the hill."

"Yes," said Prudence, "it is a hard thing for a man to go down into the Valley of Humiliation, which is where you are headed. It is difficult to go down the hill without slipping and falling, which is why we are going to accompany you down the hill."

So he began to go down, very carefully; and even with all his caution and assistance he almost slipped a time or two.

Then I saw in my dream that they all arrived at the bottom of the hill where they gave Christian a loaf of bread, a bottle of wine, and a cluster of raisins. Then Christian went on his way.

Chapter Four

A FIERCE BATTLE AND
A DARK VALLEY

nce he was in the Valley of Humiliation, poor Christian was immediately put to the test. He had not gone very far before he spied a foul fiend coming over the field to meet him. His name was Apollyon.[1]

Christian was afraid and struggled in his mind to know what he should do. Should he go back or stand his ground? As Christian thought about what to do, he realized that he had no armor for his back and that turning and running would give the enemy an easy target for his darts. Christian decided that standing his ground would give him the best chance of surviving Apollyon's attack.

So Christian went forward, and Apollyon met him. Now the monster was hideous to behold. He was clothed with scales like a fish (they are his pride), he had wings like a dragon, feet like a bear, a belly from which came fire and smoke, and the mouth of a lion. When he had advanced near Christian, he viewed him with a disdainful look and then began to question him.

Apollyon asked him, "Where did you come from? Where are you bound?"

"I came from the City of Destruction, which is the place of all evil, and I am going to the City of Zion," Christian answered.

"By your answer I perceive that you are one of my subjects, for all that country is mine, and I am the prince and god of it. How is it that you have run away from your king? Were it not for the fact that I wish you to enter into my service again, I would strike you to the ground with one blow."

Christian responded, "Indeed, I was born in your dominions, but your service was hard, and a man cannot live on the wages you pay, 'for the wages of sin is death.'[a] Therefore, when I grew into a greater understanding, I did as other thoughtful persons have done: I searched to see if there was a way to make myself into the person I should be."

To that, Apollyon protested, "There is no prince who will so easily lose his subjects, nor will I lose you. But since you complained about your service and wages, be content to go back. What our country can afford, I promise to give to you."

Christian boldly proclaimed, "But I have given myself to another, even to the King of princes, so how can I in fairness go back to you?"

"As the proverb says, you have 'changed a bad for a worse,'" Apollyon said, "but it is very common for those who have professed themselves His servants to give Him the slip after a while and return to me. And if you return to me, everything will be well with you."

Christian asserted with confidence, "I have given Him my faith and have sworn my allegiance to Him. How can I change my mind now without being hanged as a traitor?"

"You did the same to me, and yet I am willing to let it pass, if you will now turn and come back."

Christian replied, "What I promised you was done in ignorance, and besides, I believe that the Prince under whose banner I now stand is able to absolve me and to pardon me for those things I did while in your service. Besides, O you destroying Apollyon, to speak

---

[a]Romans 6:23.

down and ate some of the bread and drank from the bottle that had been given to him by Prudence, Piety, and Charity.

After Christian had refreshed himself, he began his journey again. Not knowing whether Apollyon would come back for another skirmish or whether some other enemy might be at hand, Christian drew his sword and walked carefully through the valley, but he met with no other enemies.

Now at the end of the Valley of Humiliation there was another valley, the Valley of the Shadow of Death.[5] And since there was no other way to the Celestial City, Christian was obliged to go through it.

Now this valley was a very solitary place, and as the prophet Jeremiah described it, "a wilderness, a land of deserts, and of pits, a land of drought, and of the shadow of death, a land that no man [but a Christian] passed through, and where no one lived."[e]

Now here Christian was to be afflicted more than in his fight with Apollyon, as the following adventure will show.

When Christian came to the borders of the Valley of the Shadow of Death, I saw in my dream that he met two men coming toward him, children of those men who brought an evil report concerning the good land of Canaan.[f6] These two men were quickly retreating when Christian stopped them and asked them where they were going.

They said, "Back! back! And we would advise you to do so too, if you have any concern for your life or your peace of mind."

"Why? What's the matter?" inquired Christian.

"Matter!" said they. "We were going the same way that you are now going, and we went as far as we dared to go and almost went past the point of no return. Had we continued, we would not be here to warn you."

"But what did you encounter that made you so fearful?" asked Christian.

"Why, we were almost in the Valley of the Shadow of Death, but

[e]Jeremiah 2:6.
[f]Numbers 13.

Christian walks through the Valley of the Shadow of Death.

as our good fortune would have it, we looked ahead and saw the danger before we came to it."[g]

"But what have you seen?" persisted Christian.

"Seen!" they nearly shouted. "Why, the valley itself, which is black as pitch; yet we also saw hobgoblins, satyrs, and dragons of the pit. We also heard in the valley a continual howling and yelling that sounded like people in unutterable misery who are bound in affliction and irons. Over the valley hangs the discouraging clouds of confusion. Death also spreads his wings over it. In a word, it is dreadful and completely unruly."[h][7]

Then Christian said, "All these terrors aside, nothing that you have said so far convinces me that this is anything but the way to the Celestial City."[i][8]

"Have your own way, but we will not choose it as ours."

So they parted, and Christian went on his way, with his sword in his hand, fearing he might yet be assaulted.

Then I saw in my dream that for the entire length of the valley, there was a very deep ditch on the right side. It is into this ditch that the blind have been leading the blind since the beginning of time, to the destruction of both blind leaders and their followers.[j]

I saw also on the left side of the valley a very dangerous quagmire, in which not even a good man can find solid footing or bottom if he falls in. This is the bog King David fell into, and no doubt would have been smothered, had not He who is able pulled him out.[9]

The pathway was exceedingly narrow, and good Christian was tested to his limits. For in the dark, when he tried to avoid the ditch on the one hand, he was ready to tip over into the mire on the other. Also when he sought to escape the mire, unless he was very careful, he would almost fall into the ditch.

And so Christian went on, and I heard him sigh bitterly. For besides the dangers mentioned above, the pathway was so dark that

---

[g]Psalm 44:19; 107:10.
[h]Job 3:5; 10:22.
[i]Jeremiah 2:6.
[j]Psalm 69:14–15.

often when he lifted up his foot to step forward, he never was sure where his foot would land or what he would step on.

In the middle of this valley I saw in my dream the mouth of Hell, and it stood right next to the path.[10]

What shall I do now? thought Christian. Abundant flame and smoke spewed from the place, with sparks and hideous noises (things that could not be fought with a sword, as Apollyon was). Christian put his sword back in its sheath and took out another weapon, the one called All-prayer.[k]

Then I heard Christian cry out, "O Lord, I beseech You, deliver my soul!"[l] He continued in this way for a long time, but still the flames were reaching toward him. Also he heard tortured, sad voices and the sound of things rushing and scurrying back and forth, and sometimes Christian thought he was going to be torn to pieces or trampled down like mud in the streets.

Christian saw these frightful sights and heard the dreadful noises for several miles of his journey, and, adding to his troubles, he came to a place where he thought he heard a company of fiends coming forward to meet him. Christian stopped to think about how best to meet this new enemy. For a brief moment he thought about turning back but then thought that perhaps he was halfway through the valley. He also remembered how he had already vanquished many dangers and that the danger of going back might prove worse than the dangers ahead of him. So he made up his mind to continue going forward.

The fiends seemed to be coming nearer and nearer, but when they were almost upon him, Christian cried out with a most vehement voice, "I will walk in the strength of the Lord God!" So they turned around and went back from where they came.

By this time I noticed that poor Christian was so confounded that he did not recognize his own voice. Just when he came near the mouth of the burning pit, one of the wicked ones stepped up

---

[k]Ephesians 6:18.
[l]Psalm 116:4.

softly behind him and whispered many grievous blasphemies to him, which Christian truly thought had come from his own mind. It grieved Christian more than anything that he had met with before to think that he should now blaspheme Him whom he loved, though in truth Christian had not done that. He wished to stop the wicked thought but did not have the discretion to simply plug his ears to silence the lies that a wicked one spoke to him or to recognize their source.

After Christian had traveled in this disturbing condition for some time, he thought he heard the voice of a man going before him, saying, "Though I walk through the valley of the shadow of death, I will fear no evil; for You are with me."[m]

Then Christian was glad, and for good reasons. For one, Christian believed that someone who feared God was in the valley with him. Secondly, he perceived that God was with this person up ahead, even though it was dark and dismal. Christian reasoned that if God was with this fellow traveler, then He was also with him, even though the evil in this place prevented his perception of it.[n] Thirdly, Christian hoped that he could catch up with the person ahead and have a companion on his journey.

So he went forward and called out to the pilgrim ahead of him, but this fellow traveler did not know what to answer since he thought that he was alone. Finally the sun came up on a new day, and Christian rejoiced and said, "He has 'turned the shadow of death into the morning.'"[o][11]

Then Christian looked back, not out of any desire to return, but so that he could see by the light of day what hazards he had gone through in the dark. So he saw more clearly the ditch that was on the one hand and the quagmire on the other. He also saw how narrow the way was that went between them both. He saw the hobgoblins, satyrs, and dragons of the pit, but all far-off (for after the sun came up, they would not come near). But yet they were revealed to

---

[m]Psalm 23:4.
[n]Job 9:11.
[o]Amos 5:8.

him just as it is written, "He discovers deep things out of darkness, and brings out to light the shadow of death."[p] Christian was deeply moved by his deliverance from all the dangers of the solitary way that went through the valley, dangers that he feared more before but could only now clearly see.

In the new light of day, Christian realized how treacherous the first part of his journey through the Valley of the Shadow of Death had been. But it would not compare to the dangers that lay before him, which he had yet to travel. As Christian viewed the path ahead, he saw that it was full of pits, pitfalls, deep holes, snares, traps, and false paths that led down to the pit. Christian realized what a mercy it was to have the light of day, for had it still been dark he would never in a thousand lifetimes have been able to safely reach the end of his journey through the Valley of the Shadow of Death. So as Christian watched the sun rising he said, "His candle shines upon my head, and by His light I walk through darkness."[q] It was in this light that Christian came to the end of the valley.

Now I saw in my dream that at the end of this valley lay blood, bones, ashes, and the mangled bodies of men, even of some pilgrims who had gone this way before. While I was musing about what had caused this carnage, I spied a cave where two giants, Pope and Pagan, lived in the olden days. It was their power and tyranny that had cruelly put to death the men whose bones, blood, ashes, and mangled bodies I beheld.

Christian went by this place without much danger, which made me wonder, but I have since learned that Pagan had been dead for a long while. As for the other, even though he is still alive, his advanced age and the many skirmishes of his younger days have caused him to grow crazy and stiff in his joints. Now he can do little more than sit in his cave's mouth, grinning at pilgrims as they go by and biting his nails because he can no longer capture and destroy them.

---

[p]Job 12:22.
[q]Job 29:3.

Faithful responded, "When I left, Pliable had been the object of derision ever since he returned to the city. Many mocked and despised him and would not share his company any longer. He is seven times worse off than if he had never left the city."

Christian asked, "But why do they despise him since they also despise the way that he forsook?"

Faithful explained, "They say, 'Hang him, he is a turncoat; he was not true to his profession.' I think God has stirred up even his enemies to hiss at him and make him a proverb because he has forsaken the way."[a]

"Did you talk with him before you left on your journey?"

"I met him once in the streets," Faithful said, "but he looked the other way, ashamed of what he had done, so I did not speak with him."

Christian added, "Well, when I first started my journey, I had hopes for that man; but now I fear he will perish in the overthrow of the city. For it has happened to him according to the true proverb, 'The dog has returned to his own vomit; and the sow that was washed has returned to wallow in the mire.'"[b]

"I fear you are right. But who can prevent what is to come?" Faithful stated plaintively.

"Well, neighbor Faithful," said Christian, "let's talk of things that are of more immediate concern. Tell me, what have you met with on this journey? I would be very surprised to hear that you had undergone no adventures along the way."

"I escaped the Swamp of Despond, which I understand you fell into, and I got to the sheep gate without any danger. But I did meet with someone whose name was Wanton, who would have liked very much to harm me," Faithful reported.

"It was good you escaped her trap. Joseph was pursued by her, and he escaped her, but it almost cost him his life.[c] But what did she do to you?"

---

[a]Jeremiah 29:18–19.
[b]2 Peter 2:22.
[c]Genesis 39:11–13.

Faithful answered, "You can hardly imagine what a flattering tongue she had. She worked hard to turn me away from the path in order to go with her, promising me all sorts of fleshly pleasures and contentment."

"I am sure there is one pleasure she could not promise you—a good conscience."

"Yes, you know what I mean, all carnal and fleshly pleasures," Faithful agreed.

Christian added, "Thank God you have escaped her. The one with whom the Lord is angry will fall into her deep pit."[d]

"Well, I don't know if I completely escaped her or not."

"How is that?" Christian inquired. "I hope you did not consent to her desires."

"No," Faithful assured him, "I did not defile myself, for I remembered an old writing that I had seen that said, 'Her steps follow the path to Hell.'[e] So I shut my eyes so that I would not be bewitched with her seductive appearance.[f] Then she cursed me and abused me with her tongue, and I went on my way."

"Did you meet with any other assaults on your journey?"

Faithful recounted, "When I came to the foot of the hill called Difficulty, I met a very old man who asked me my name and destination. I told him that I was a pilgrim, going to the Celestial City. Then the old man said to me, 'You look like an honest fellow. Would you be willing to come and live with and work for me for the wages that I would be willing to give you?'

"Then I asked him his name and where he lived. He said his name was Adam the First and that he lived in the town of Deceit.[g]

"I then asked him what sort of work he had for me to do and what were the wages he would pay. He told me that his work included many delights, and for wages he would make me the heir to his estate.

---

[d]Proverbs. 22:14.
[e]Proverbs 5:5.
[f]Job 31:1.
[g]Ephesians 4:22.

"I further asked him what sort of house he lived in and what other servants he had. So he told me that his house was maintained with all the dainties in the world and that his servants were all relatives of his. Then I asked if he had any children. He said that he had but three daughters: Lust of the Flesh, Lust of the Eyes, and Pride of Life.[h] Then he told me that I could marry them all if I wished. Then I asked for how long a time he would have me live with him. And he told me that I would live with him as long as he lived."

"What was the outcome of this discussion?" Christian asked.

"Why, at first I found myself somewhat inclined to go with the man, for I thought that his offer sounded very good," Faithful said. "But as I looked at his forehead and spoke with him, I saw written, 'Put off the old man with his deeds.'"

"And then what happened?"

"Then it came rushing into my mind that despite his flattering words, he would sell me as a slave when we got to his home," Faithful said. "So I asked him to stop talking, and I told him I would not come near the door to his house.

"Then he cursed me and told me that he would send someone after me who would make my soul bitter. So I turned to go away from him, but just as I turned to go, I felt him take hold of my flesh and give me such a deadly pinch that I thought he had pulled a part of me off for himself. This made me shriek, 'Oh, wretched man!'[i] So I went on my way up the Hill Difficulty.

"Now when I had climbed about halfway up, I looked behind and saw someone coming after me, swift as the wind. Soon he overtook me just about the place where the arbor stands."

"That is the place," said Christian, "where I sat down to rest, fell asleep, and lost my scroll."

"Dear brother, hear me out," Faithful urged. "So as soon as the man overtook me, without saying a word, he struck me and knocked me down unconscious. When I came to, I asked him why he had

---

[h]1 John 2:16.
[i]Romans 7:24.

thus assaulted me. He said that it was because of my secret inclination to follow Adam the First, and with that he struck me with another deadly blow on the chest and beat me down backward, and I lay at his feet as if I were dead. So when I came to, I cried to him for mercy. But he said, 'I do not know how to show mercy' and with that knocked me down again. He would have beaten me to death, except One came by and told him to stop."

"Who was it that told him to stop?"

Faithful went on, "I did not recognize Him at first, but as He went by I saw the wounds in His hands and in His side. Then I concluded that He was our Lord. So I continued up the hill."

Christian then explained, "The man who overtook you was Moses. He spares no one, and he does not know how to show mercy to anyone who transgresses his law."

"I know that very well. It was not the first time that he had met with me. He was the one who came to me when I lived securely at home and who told me he would burn my house over my head if I stayed there."

Christian asked, "But didn't you see the house that stood on the top of the hill, on the side of the hill where Moses met you?"

Faithful answered, "Yes, and I saw the lions also, before I came near the house. But I think they were asleep, for it was about noon. Because I had so much of the day ahead of me, I passed by the porter and came down the hill."

"Yes, the porter told me that he saw you go by," Christian said. "I wish you had visited the house, for they would have shown you many rarities that you would have remembered the rest of your life. But tell me, did you meet anyone in the Valley of Humiliation?"

Faithful responded, "Yes, I met someone named Discontent who would have gladly persuaded me to go back with him. His reasoning was that the valley was altogether without honor. He told me that if I went into the valley I would be disobeying all my friends, such as Pride, Arrogance, Self-conceit, Worldly-Glory, and others he knew.

Chapter Six

A Faith Beyond Words

Now I saw in my dream that as they went on, Faithful looked to one side and saw a man whose name was Talkative[1] walking beside them a short distance away. For on that part of the path there was room enough for many to walk together. Talkative was a tall man and looked more handsome at a distance than he did up close. Faithful spoke to Talkative.

"Friend, how are you?" Faithful inquired. "Are you going to the heavenly country?"

"That is exactly where I am going," Talkative replied.

Faithful responded, "Very good. I hope we may have the pleasure of your company."

"I would be happy to be your companion on the journey."

"Come then, let's go together and spend our time in conversation about things that are excellent," Faithful invited.

Talkative said, "I am glad to have met someone who realizes how profitable it is to talk about good things. To tell you the truth, there are very few of us who will spend their time during travels speaking about what is good. Most men will waste their time talking about things that are of no value, a fact that troubles me."

Faithful agreed, "Yes, that waste of time is something to regret.

Is there anything more worthy of our tongues and mouths than to speak of the things of God and Heaven?"

"I'm enjoying your company already," Talkative said warmly. "Your speech is full of conviction. And to what you said I would add that there is nothing more profitable or pleasant as talking about the things of God. Also, if a man likes to talk about history, or the mystery of things, or miracles, or signs and wonders, where would he find it recorded more sweetly than in the Holy Scripture?"

Faithful agreed, saying, "That is true. We should desire to thus be profited in our conversation by purposely talking about the things of God."

Talkative added, "Those are my thoughts also, for to talk of such things is most profitable. By so doing, a man may gain knowledge about many things, including the vanity of earthly things and the benefit of things above. To be more specific, by talking a man may learn the necessity of the new birth, the insufficiency of our works, the need of Christ's righteousness, etc.

"In addition, by talking a man may learn what it is to repent, to believe, to pray, to suffer, and the like. By talking a man may learn what are the great promises and consolations of the gospel and be comforted by those promises. Further, by talking a man may learn to refute false opinions, to defend the truth, and also to instruct the ignorant."

"All this is true, and glad am I to hear you say them," Faithful stated.

Talkative went on, "Because there is so little talk of these things, there are few who understand the need for faith and the necessity of a work of grace in their soul for the obtaining of eternal life. They still ignorantly live by the works of the Law, through which no man may by any means obtain the Kingdom of Heaven."

Faithful said, "Yes, but the heavenly knowledge of these things is the gift of God. No man can attain them by human industry or by merely talking about them."

"All this I know very well," Talkative said softly. "For a man discourse about the power of religion, which he will affirm, I assure you. Then ask him plainly whether this power is something that is truly working itself out in his heart and in his home and in his behavior."

So Faithful stepped back over to where Talkative was walking and began to converse with him. "How are you doing?" he asked.

"Very well, thank you," Talkative replied. "I thought we should have had a great deal of talk by now."

Faithful offered, "If you would like, we will continue our conversation. And when we last spoke, you left it to me to pose a topic for discussion. Here is my question: how does the saving grace of God make itself known when it is in the heart of man?"

"I see," Talkative stated. "You want to talk about the power of things. Well, that is a very good question, and I will be happy to answer you. I will make my answer brief and to the point. First, where the grace of God is at work in the heart, it causes there to be a great outcry against sin. Secondly—"

Faithful interjected, "Wait a minute. Let's consider your points one at a time. I think you should have said, 'It makes itself known by inclining the soul to abhor its sin.'"[4]

"Why, what is the difference between crying out against and abhorring sin?" Talkative inquired.

Faithful answered, "There is a great deal of difference. A man may cry out against sin out of principle, but he cannot abhor it unless he has God's own antipathy against it. For instance, I have seen many cry out against sin in the pulpit who yet abide it well enough in their own heart, home, and manner of life.

"Potiphar's wife cried out against Joseph with a loud voice, as if she had been very holy. Yet she would have gladly, despite her cries to the contrary, committed adultery with him.[h] Some cry out against sin as a mother cries out against her child, when she calls her a good-for-nothing and a naughty girl and then smothers her with hugs and kisses."

---

[h]Genesis 39:15.

"I think you're trying to trip me up with details," Talkative accused.

Faithful responded, "No, I am only trying to set things right. But what is the second way in which a work of grace makes itself known in the heart of man?"

"Great knowledge of gospel mysteries," Talkative offered.

Faithful countered, "This sign should have been first, but first or last, it is also false. For knowledge, even great knowledge, may be obtained in the mysteries of the gospel without a work of grace in the soul.[i] The truth is that a man can have an abundance of knowledge and still be nothing, and so consequently, no child of God.

"When Christ asked, 'Do you know all these things?' and the disciples answered, 'Yes,' He added, 'Blessed are you if you do them.'[j] He did not pronounce a blessing for knowing but for doing. For there is a knowledge that is not connected with doing: 'he that knows his master's will, and does not do it.' A man may know like an angel and yet not be a Christian. Therefore the point you make is not true.

"Indeed, to know is something that pleases talkers and boasters, but to do is that which pleases God. Not that the heart can be good without knowledge, for without knowledge the heart is empty. But there are two kinds of knowledge: the first is alone in its bare speculation of things, and the second is accompanied by the grace of faith and love, which causes a man to do the will of God from the heart.

"The first kind of knowledge will serve the talker. But a true Christian will not be content until his knowledge results in sincere works that please God. 'Give me understanding, and I shall keep Thy law; yea, I shall observe it with my whole heart.'"[k]

Talkative protested, "You are trying to trap me again; this is not edifying."

"Well then, tell me another way in which the saving grace of

---

[i]1 Corinthians 13.
[j]John 13:17.
[k]Psalm 119:34.

God makes itself known when it is in the heart of man," Faithful challenged.

"Not I, for I see we shall not agree."

Faithful offered, "Well, if you will not, may I have your permission to do it?"

"You are free to say whatever you want," Talkative said.

Faithful began, "A work of grace in the soul makes itself known either to the one who has it or to onlookers.

"Where God's grace is truly at work, it produces conviction of sin as the converted soul becomes aware of the defilement of his nature and the sin of unbelief (a sin that he now knows with certainty will send him to Hell unless he finds mercy at God's hand by faith in Jesus Christ).[l]

"This new awakening of the soul works in him to produce a sorrow and shame for sin, but that is not all. He also finds revealed in him the Savior of the world and realizes the absolute necessity of clinging to Him for life. When he desperately clutches onto Him, the awakened soul finds that his hunger and thirst for the Savior increases just as it is promised.[m] Now, according to the strength or weakness of his faith in his Savior, so is his joy and peace, so is his love for holiness, so are his desires to know Him more and to serve Him more single-mindedly in this present world.

"But although I say that this work of grace is partially discovered by the sinner, yet it is very seldom that he is able to conclude that this is a work of grace. Because of the corruptions of his earthly nature and the continued faultiness of his reason, he is likely to misjudge the work that is going on inside of him. Therefore, in him who has this grace, there is required very sound judgment before he can, with some assurance, conclude that this is a work of God's grace.

"To others it is made known as follows:

"1. By a confession of his faith in Christ.[n]

---

[l]John 16:8; Romans 7:24; John 16:9; Mark 16:16.
[m]Psalm 38:18; Jeremiah 31:19; Galatians 2:16; Acts 4:12; Matthew 5:6; Revelation 21:6.
[n]Romans 10:10; Philippians 1:27; Matthew 5:19.

"2. By a life that is answerable to that confession. To be specific, a life of holiness: heart-holiness, family-holiness (if he has a family), and by life and conversation sharply distinguished from the world. Such a man inwardly abhors both his sin and himself for sinning, suppresses sin in his family, and promotes holiness in the world. He does not do this by talk only, as a hypocrite or talkative person may do, but by a practical demonstration of a godly life, in faith and love, through the power of the Word.°

"If you have no objection to this brief description of the work of grace and how it evidences itself in the life of a true believer, then I will ask you a second question."

Talkative calmly stated, "My part is not to object, but to listen. Let me hear your second question."

Faithful went on, "It is this: have you experienced what I have described? Do your life and your conduct testify to prove it? Or does your religion consist of words only, without deeds to attest to the truth of them?

"Please, if you want to answer me, be careful to say no more than what you know God above will say Amen to. Say nothing that your conscience would not approve. 'For it is not the one who commends himself who is approved, but the one whom the Lord commends.'ᴾ Besides, it is great wickedness to say, 'I am such and such' when my conduct and all my neighbors say completely otherwise."

Then Talkative began to blush but quickly recovered and said, "You talk now about experience, conscience, and God. You appeal to Him for justification of what is spoken. This is not the kind of discourse I expected, nor am I disposed to give an answer to such questions, nor do I feel obligated to answer, unless you are taking on the job of a catechism teacher. Even if that is how you see yourself, I refuse to allow you to become my judge. But I would be interested in why you ask me such questions."

Faithful responded, "Because you were so anxious to talk and

°John 14:15; Psalm 1:2–3; Job 42:5–6; Ezekiel 20:43.
ᴾ2 Corinthians 10:18, ᴇsᴠ.

happened to them since they last met and of all the difficulties that had brought them to where they now were.

"I am glad," said Evangelist, "not that you have met with trials, but that you have been victors and that you have been faithful despite your many weaknesses and troubles along the way.[3] I am glad for your sakes and for mine. I have sowed, and you have reaped. The day is coming when both he who sowed and they who reaped shall rejoice together. That is, of course, if you endure to the end, 'for in due season we shall reap, if we do not give up.'[a] The crown is before you, and it is an incorruptible one; 'so run, that you may obtain' it.[b]

"Some who set out for this crown, even after they have gone quite a long ways, allow others who come along to snatch their victory from them. So hold fast to what you have, and let no man take away your crown.[c] You are not yet out of reach of the gunshot of the Devil. You have not yet resisted unto death in your striving against sin. Let the Kingdom be always before you, and believe with certainty and consistency the things that are yet unseen. Let nothing that is on this side of eternal life get inside you. Above all, take care of your own hearts, and resist the lusts that tempt you, for your hearts 'are deceitful above all things, and desperately wicked.'[d] Set your faces like a flint; you have all the power of Heaven and earth on your side."

Christian thanked Evangelist for his exhortation. Then Christian and Faithful asked him to speak of more, knowing that he was a prophet. They hoped to hear from Evangelist things that would help them resist and overcome trials they were likely to encounter as they continued their journey.

Evangelist consented to their request and began to speak to them.

"My sons, you have heard in the words of the gospel that you must go through many tribulations before you enter the Kingdom of Heaven, and also that in every city you enter, bonds and afflictions await you. Therefore, you cannot expect to travel too long on

---

[a]John 4:36; Galatians 6:9.
[b]1 Corinthians 9:24–27.
[c]Revelation 3:11.
[d]Jeremiah 17:9.

your pilgrimage without suffering tribulation. You have discovered the truth of these testimonies in the struggles you have already endured, and more will immediately follow.

"You are almost out of this wilderness and will very soon see the town you will enter next on your journey.[4] In that town you will be set upon by enemies who will be determined to kill you and who will succeed. You can be sure that one or both of you must seal his testimony with blood. So be faithful unto death, and the King will give you a crown of life. The one who dies there, although his death will be unnatural and perhaps very painful, will be better off than his companion, not only because he will arrive at the Celestial City sooner, but also because he will escape many of the miseries that the other will meet with on the rest of his journey.

"So when you come to the town and this happens to you, fulfilling what I have related, then remember me and the things that I have told you. Conduct yourselves like men, and commit the keeping of your souls to your God as you struggle to do what is right. Remember that He is your faithful Creator."

Then I saw in my dream that when they had left the borders of the wilderness, they immediately saw a town before them. The name of that town is Vanity, and in the town there is a year-round market called Vanity Fair. It bears its name because the town that hosts the fair is only concerned with things that are unimportant and vain. All that is bought and sold at the fair is likewise vain and worthless. As the ancient saying goes, 'All that cometh is vanity.'[e] This fair is no new business but has been established from ancient times. I will now explain to you its history and origins.

Almost five thousand years ago, there were pilgrims walking to the Celestial City, just as Christian and Faithful were doing. Beelzebub, Apollyon, and Legion, with their companions, seeing that the pilgrims' path went right through the town of Vanity, conspired together to set up a fair in which all sorts of vain merchandise were sold all year long. This merchandise consisted of

---

[e]Ecclesiastes 1; 2:11, 17; 11:8; Isaiah 40:17.

houses, lands, trades, places, honors, positions, titles, countries, kingdoms, lusts, pleasures, and delights of all sorts, such as whores, lewd entertainment, wives, husbands, children, masters, servants, lives, blood, bodies, souls, silver, gold, pearls, precious stones, and whatnot. Moreover, at this fair can always be seen juggling, cheats, games, plays, fools, apes, knaves, and rogues, and that of every kind. Also to be seen, and at no charge, are thefts, murders, adulteries, and false witnesses who cause death with their lies.

As in other fairs of less importance, where there are several rows and streets all properly named for the different wares that are vended, so also Vanity Fair has the proper places, rows, streets (countries and kingdoms) where the wares of this fair can be found. Here is the Britain Row, the French Row, the Italian Row, the Spanish Row, the German Row, where various sorts of vanities are to be sold. Also as in other fairs, where one particular commodity is in great demand, so it is in Vanity Fair. Here the ware of Rome is greatly promoted and desired, and only a few nations, including England, have taken a dislike to the goods of Rome.

Now as I said, the way to the Celestial City lies just through this town where this lusty fair is kept. Anyone going to the Celestial City who will not go through this town must "go out of the world."[f] The Prince of princes Himself, when He was here, went through this town to His own country. I think it was Beelzebub, the chief lord of this fair, who invited Him to buy some of his vanities. He even offered to make Him lord of the fair if only He would show him reverence as He went through the town.[g] Because the Prince was such a person of honor, Beelzebub took Him from street to street and showed Him all the kingdoms of the world in a little time in order to, if possible, allure the Blessed One to cheapen Himself and buy some of his vanities. But the Prince had no interest in the merchandise and left the town without spending so much as one penny on anything there.

---

[f] 1 Corinthians 5:10.
[g] Matthew 4:8; Luke 4:5–7.

Christian and Faithful enter Vanity Fair.

This fair is a great, ancient, and long-standing place. Now these pilgrims, as I said, must pass through this Vanity Fair. And so they did, but as they entered into the fair, they created a great commotion, and all the people in the fair turned their attention to the two pilgrims.[5]

There were several reasons for this:

First, the pilgrims were dressed differently from the people trading at the fair. The people of the fair looked at them in astonishment. Some said they were fools, some said they were lunatics, and some said they were just outlandish men.[h6]

Secondly, as strange as the pilgrims' attire appeared to their onlookers, their speech was judged even stranger. Very few could even understand what the pilgrims said since they spoke the language of the promised Kingdom rather than the language of the world, which was the common language of the fair. So from one end of the fair to the other, they seemed like barbarians to the others.

Thirdly, the thing that most annoyed and puzzled the merchants was that these pilgrims put no value on the fair's goods. They did not even enjoy looking at them, and when the merchants called out to them to buy this or that, the pilgrims put their fingers in their ears and cried out, "Turn away mine eyes from beholding vanity" and looked upward, signifying that their trade and traffic was in Heaven.[i]

One merchant, observing the strange conduct of the pilgrims, mockingly said to them, "What will you buy?"

But they, looking sternly at him, answered, "We buy the truth."[j]

This caused great offense, and the merchants began to despise the pilgrims even more. Some mocked, some taunted, some spoke reproachfully, and some began to call out for others to strike them. Finally the pilgrims created so much commotion that the natural order of the fair was disrupted. The confusion was so great that word was sent to the Great One of the fair, who quickly came down

---

[h]1 Corinthians 2:6–8.
[i]Psalm 119:37; Philippians 3:19–20.
[j]Proverbs 23:23.

and dispatched a few of his most trusted friends to detain and question the two pilgrims.

So they were held and questioned. The men who examined them asked them where they came from, where they were going, and why they dressed in such unusual garb.

Christian and Faithful told them that they were pilgrims and strangers in the world and that they were going to their own country, which was the Heavenly Jerusalem.[k] They also told them that they had done nothing to the men or the merchants of the town that should have caused them to be so mistreated and detained from making progress on their journey. The only thing they did that caused an offense was to tell those who were trying to sell them their wares that they would only buy the truth.

The men who were appointed to examine Christian and Faithful concluded that they were either mad vagabonds or else troublemakers who had come to create confusion in the fair.

So they took them, beat them, smeared them with dirt, and then put them into a cage to be a spectacle to all the men of the fair. There they stayed for some time, the objects of ridicule, malice, or revenge for any passerby who wished to abuse them, which caused the Great One of the fair to laugh viciously at their plight.

But the pilgrims remained calm and patient. When men would come to yell and scream every sort of vile abuse at them, they responded with kind words. When men came and cursed them, they in turn blessed them, returning good words for bad and kindness for injuries.

Some men who were more thoughtful and less prejudiced than the rest began to criticize and rebuke the more brutish men of the crowd for their continual abuse of the two pilgrims. This caused a heated reaction to the pilgrims' would-be defenders who were called traitors and confederates of the caged men. Some in the mob said that those who defended the pilgrims should suffer their misfortune.

[k]Hebrews 11:13–16.

The more reasonable men replied that as far as they could see, the pilgrims were quiet and sober and intended nobody any harm. They also noted that many who traded in the fair were more worthy to be put into the cage than these two.

So after many angry words had passed on both sides, they began to fight among themselves, causing many injuries. While all this was happening, the two pilgrims conducted themselves with dignity and wisdom.

But after this incident the two poor pilgrims were brought before their examiners again and were charged with inciting a riot in the fair. So the authorities beat them without mercy, shackled them with irons, and led them in chains up and down the fair. This was done to frighten anyone who was thinking about speaking up on their behalf or joining their cause.

Throughout the whole spectacle, Christian and Faithful behaved themselves wisely and received the ignominy and shame that was cast upon them with so much meekness and patience that it won to their side a few men even in that fair. This put the other party into an even greater rage, so much so that they decided that the cage and the irons were not punishment enough: the two pilgrims should be put to death for all the abuse they had caused and for deluding the men of the fair. So Christian and Faithful were returned to the cage again with their feet in stocks until further plans for their execution could be made.

While enduring all this persecution, Christian and Faithful remembered what their faithful friend Evangelist had told them about the suffering that would happen to them. This strengthened their resolve to bear all the abuse and await patiently the outcome of their situation. They also reminded one another for their mutual comfort that whichever one of them suffered death would have the best outcome. Therefore each secretly hoped that he might be the one chosen for that fate. Nevertheless, each committed himself to the wise plans of Him who rules all things, and so they were content to remain in their current condition until it should please God to use them otherwise.

Then at the appointed time they were led to their trial, which was planned with only one purpose in mind—the condemnation of them both. First they were brought before their enemies and formally charged. The judge's name was Lord Hate-Good. Their indictments were the same in substance, though somewhat varying in form. The contents were as follows: "That they were enemies to, and disturbers of, trade; that they had made commotions and divisions in the town and had won a faction over to their own most dangerous opinions, in contempt of the law of the prince."

Faithful was the first to be put on trial, and he began his defense by saying that he had only set himself against the enemy of Him who is higher than the highest. And he said, "As for disturbance, I made none, for I am a man of peace. The individuals who were won over to our side were won by seeing the truth and our innocence, and they are better off for it. And as to the king you talk of, since he is Beelzebub, the enemy of our Lord, I defy him and all his angels."

Then proclamation was made that those who wished to bring accusations against the prisoners should be brought forth to present their evidence on behalf of their king.

Three witnesses came—Envy, Superstition, and Flattery. They were then asked if they knew the prisoners and what they had to say against them on behalf of the lord their king.

Then Envy stood up and said, "My lord, I have known this man a long time and will attest upon my oath before this honorable bench that he is—"

"Hold," the judge interjected. "Give him his oath." (So they swore him in.)

Then Envy continued, "My lord, this man, notwithstanding his innocent name, is one of the vilest men in our country. He does not regard prince or people, law or custom, but does all that he can to instill in others his disloyal notions, which he generally calls 'principles of faith and holiness.' In particular, I heard him with my own

Faithful is on trial in Vanity Fair.

ears affirm that Christianity and the customs of our town of Vanity were diametrically opposed and cannot be reconciled. And by saying that, my lord, he condemns all the laudable things we do and us in the same breath."

Then the judge said to Envy, "Do you have any more to say?"

Envy loudly asserted, "My lord, I could say much more if it would not be so tedious to the court. Yet, if need be, when the other gentlemen have presented their evidence, if anything is missing that would guarantee the condemnation of the prisoners, I will enlarge my testimony against them at that time."

So he was told to stand by.

Then they called Superstition and asked him to look upon the prisoner. They also asked what he could say for their lord the king against him. After he took his oath, he began.

"My lord, I have no real acquaintance with this man, nor do I desire to have any further knowledge of him. However, after having a conversation with him the other day, I can report that he is a very dangerous fellow. I heard him say that our religion was useless and unable to show man any way to please God. We all know that this is the same as saying that we worship in vain, have no forgiveness of our sins, and face damnation. This is what I have to say to the court."

Then Flattery was sworn in and was asked to say what he knew against the prisoner, on behalf of their lord the king.

"My lord and all the rest of you gentlemen, I have known of this fellow for a long time. I have heard him say things that should not be said. He has reviled and scolded in the harshest terms our noble prince Beelzebub and has spoken contemptibly of the prince's honorable friends, whose names are the Lord Old Man, the Lord Carnal Delight, the Lord Luxurious, the Lord Desire of Vain-Glory, Lord Lechery, and Sir Greed, along with all the rest of our nobility. He has also said that if all men were of his mind, there is not one of these noblemen who would not be driven out of our town. Besides, he has not been afraid to rail against you, my lord, who are now appointed to be his judge, calling you an ungodly villain and many other such vilifying terms, with which he has sullied most of the gentry of our town."

When Flattery had finished telling his tale, the judge directed his speech to the prisoner at the bar saying, "You renegade, heretic, and traitor, have you heard what these honest gentlemen have witnessed against you?"

"May I speak a few words in my own defense?" Faithful asked.

The judge protested, "What! What! You deserve to live no longer but to be slain immediately on this very spot! But so that everyone may see our gentleness toward you, let us hear what you have to say."

Faithful began, "In the first place, in answer to what Mr. Envy has said, I never said anything but the following: whatever rules or laws or customs or peoples are contrary to the Word of God, these things are diametrically opposed to Christianity. If I have said something wrong, then convince me of my error, and I am ready here, before you all, to make my recantation.

"As to the second point that Mr. Superstition made and his charge against me, I said only this: in the worship of God there is required a divine faith that only attends a divine revelation of the will of God. Therefore, whatever things are thrust into the worship of God that are contrary to divine revelation cannot be done but by mere human faith, and human faith will not result in eternal life.

"As to what Mr. Flattery has charged, I said (without ranting) that the prince of this town, his attendants, the brutish mob, and all the rest named by Mr. Flattery are more ready for Hell than for this town and country. And so, may the Lord have mercy upon me!"

Then the judge called to the jurymen (who were standing by and had observed all that had been said and done), "Gentlemen of the jury, you see this man about whom so great an uproar has been made in this town. You have also heard what these worthy gentlemen have witnessed against him. Also you have heard his reply and confession. It is now your responsibility to hang him or save his life. But before you decide, I think I need to instruct you in our law. There was an Act made in the days of Pharaoh the Great, servant to our prince, that to prevent those of a contrary religion from multiplying and growing too strong, the male children of those troublesome people should be drowned in the river.[l]

"There was also an Act made in the days of Nebuchadnezzar the Great, another of our lord's servants, that whoever would not fall down and worship his golden image should be thrown into a fiery furnace.[m]

"There was also an Act made in the days of Darius that anyone who called upon any god except for him should be cast into the lions' den.[n] Now this rebel before you has broken the substance of these laws, not only in thought but also in word and deed. This is intolerable.

"Consider that the law made by Pharaoh was made to prevent mischief, no crime having yet been committed. But here before you is a crime apparent. As far as the second and third laws I told you of, you can see for yourself that he disputes against our religion, and for the treason he has confessed he deserves to die by execution."

After hearing all this, the jury went to private quarters to deliberate. The jurors' names were Mr. Blind-man, Mr. No-good, Mr. Malice, Mr. Love-lust, Mr. Live-loose, Mr. Hothead, Mr. High-mind, Mr. Enmity, Mr. Liar, Mr. Cruelty, Mr. Hate-light, Mr. Implacable.

Each one submitted his private verdict against Faithful to the other jurors, and after that, they unanimously concluded to bring a verdict of "guilty" against Faithful.

They went before the judge with their verdict. The first juror to speak was Mr. Blind-man, the foreman, who said, "I see clearly that this man is a heretic."

Then Mr. No-good said, "Away with such a fellow from the earth!"

"I agree," said Mr. Malice, "for I hate the very looks of him."

Then Mr. Love-lust said, "I could never stand the sight of him."

[l]Exodus 1.
[m]Daniel 3.
[n]Daniel 6.

"Nor I," said Mr. Live-loose, "for he would always be condemning me."

"Hang him, hang him!" said Mr. Hothead.

"A sorry vermin," said Mr. High-mind.

"My heart rises against him," said Mr. Enmity.

"He is a rogue," said Mr. Liar.

"Hanging is too good for him!" said Mr. Cruelty.

"Let us kill him quickly and get him out of the way," said Mr. Hate-light.

Then said Mr. Implacable, "Even if I was offered all the world to make peace with this man, I could not. Therefore, let us quickly bring in a guilty verdict and put him to death."

And so they did. Faithful was condemned and was taken to a place where he was put to the most cruel death they could invent. First they scourged him, then they beat him, then they lanced his flesh with knives. After that, they stoned him with stones and pierced him with their swords. Last of all, they burned him to ashes at the stake. This is how Faithful came to his end.

Now I saw in my dream that there stood behind this brutal multitude a chariot and a couple of horses, waiting for Faithful. So as soon as his adversaries had killed him, he was taken into it and was immediately carried up through the clouds, with the sound of trumpets, heading straightaway to the Celestial Gate.

But as for Christian, he had a temporary delay and was returned to prison where he stayed for some time. But He who overrules all things, having the power of even His enemies' rage in His own hand, brought about Christian's escape from their evil plans. So Christian went on his way, singing:

> *"Well, Faithful, thou hast faithfully professed*
> *Unto thy Lord, with whom thou shalt be blessed.*
> *When faithless ones, with all their vain delights,*
> *Are crying out under their hellish plights,*
> *Sing, Faithful, sing, and let thy name survive;*
> *For though they killed thee, thou art yet alive."*

Faithful departs to the Celestial City.

Now I saw in my dream that Christian did not escape Vanity Fair by himself, for there was with him a man named Hopeful (a name he was given as he watched how Christian and Faithful in their words and in their deeds conducted themselves during all their sufferings at the fair).[7]

Hopeful had joined himself to Christian and entered into a brotherly covenant with him, promising him that he would be his companion for the rest of the journey.

So one died to bear testimony to the truth, and another rose out of his ashes to be a companion with Christian in his pilgrimage. Hopeful also told Christian there were many more men in the fair who would in due course follow after them to the Celestial City.

Chapter Eight

Confronting Worldly Attachments

So I saw in my dream that soon after they had left the fair, they overtook a man walking ahead of them whose name was By-ends. So they said to him, "What country are you from, sir, and how far you going on this way?" He told them that he came from the town of Fair-speech and that he was going to the Celestial City, but he did not tell them his name.[1]

"From Fair-speech!"[2] exclaimed Christian. "Does anything good live there?"[a]

"Yes, I hope so," said By-ends.

"Please, sir, what is your name?" inquired Christian.

By-ends answered, "I am a stranger to you, and you to me, but if you are going this way, I shall be glad of your company. If not, I must be content to walk alone."

"I have heard of this town of Fair-speech," said Christian, "and, as I remember, they say it is a wealthy place."

By-ends agreed, "Yes, I will assure you that it is, and I have many rich relatives who live there."

[a]Proverbs 26:25.

"May I be so bold as to ask who some of your relatives are who live there?" Christian asked.

By-ends reported, "Almost the whole town is related to me, and in particular Lord Turn-about, Lord Time-server, and Lord Fair-speech (from whose ancestors that town first took its name). Other relatives include Mr. Smooth-man, Mr. Facing-both-ways, and Mr. Anything. The parson of our parish, Mr. Two-tongues, is my uncle on my mother's side. And to tell you the truth, I have become a gentleman of good quality, even though my great-grandfather was only a ferryman, looking one way and rowing another. I earned most of my wealth by the same occupation."

Christian asked, "Are you a married man?"

By-ends replied, "Yes, and my wife is a very virtuous woman, the daughter of a virtuous woman. She was my Lady Feigning's daughter. She comes from a very honorable family and has arrived to such a pinnacle of breeding that she knows how to act cordially and respectably to all, princes and peasants alike.

"It is true that we differ in religion from those of the stricter sort, but only in two small points. First, we never strive against the wind and tide. Secondly, we are always most zealous when religion goes about in his silver slippers. We love to walk with him in the street if the sun is shining and the people are applauding him."[3]

Then Christian stepped aside to his friend Hopeful and said, "I believe this is the person they call By-ends of Fair-speech. If it is he, then we have in our company one of the most deceitful rogues who ever lived in this part of the country."[4]

Then Hopeful said, "Ask him. I do not think he should be ashamed of his name."

So Christian came up to him again and said, "Sir, you talk as if you knew more than most people in the world, and if I am not mistaken, I would guess that your name is Mr. By-ends of Fair-speech."

By-ends protested, "That is not my name, but it *is* an insulting nickname that has been given to me by those who do not care for me. I must be content to bear it as a reproach, as other good men have borne theirs before me."

"But haven't you given occasion for men to call you by this name?" Christian pressed.

"Never! Never!" By-ends protested. "The worst thing I ever did to invite such a name was to have the good luck to jump in and ride the tide of the times, profiting thereby from my skill at knowing which way the winds of change were blowing. If this is my crime, then I will count it a blessing. But I will not let the malicious load me up with reproach."

Christian responded, "Just as I thought, you are the man of whom I heard, and to tell you the truth, I fear your nickname belongs to you more properly than you would like us to think."

By-ends countered, "Well, if this is what you think, I cannot help it. Even so, you will find me to be good company if you will still allow me to travel with you."

Christian replied, "If you will go with us, you must go against wind and tide, which I believe is against your principles. You must also stand by religion in his rags as well as when he is in his silver slippers. You must stand by him when he is bound in irons as well as when he walks the streets and hears applause."

"You must not impose your faith on me. Let me have my views, and let me go with you," By-ends implored.

Christian insisted, "Not a step further unless you will do as I have just proposed, even as we do."

Then By-ends said, "I will never desert my old principles since they are harmless and profitable. If I may not go with you, then I must do what I did before you caught up to me, which is to go by myself until someone overtakes me who will be glad for my company."

Now I saw in my dream that Christian and Hopeful forsook him and kept a good distance ahead of him.

After a while Christian looked back and saw three men fol-lowing Mr. By-ends. And as they came up to him, he greeted them with a low bow, and they gave him a compliment. The men's names were Mr. Hold-the-world, Mr. Money-love, and Mr. Save-all.[5] These were men with whom Mr. By-ends had formerly been acquainted, for in their youth they were schoolfellows and were taught by one Mr. Gripe-man. They had gone to school in Love-gain, which is a market town in the county of Coveting to the north.

This schoolmaster taught them the art of getting, either by violence, fraud, flattery, lying, or putting on a guise of religion. And these four gentlemen had become so proficient in the art of their master that now each of them had his own school.

When they had all greeted each other, Mr. Money-love said to Mr. By-ends, "Who are they upon the road ahead of us?" (for Christian and Hopeful were yet within view).

By-ends responded, "They are a pair from a far-off country going on pilgrimage in their own way."

Money-love asked, "Why didn't they stay with you so that we might have had their good company? For they and we, sir, are all going on a pilgrimage."

"So we are," By-ends said. "But the men before us are rigid and in love with their own notions. They disdain the opinions of others, with a superior attitude that is so narrow that if you don't agree with them in all things, they throw you out of their company."

Save-all commented, "That is bad. I have read about those who become overzealous in righteousness, judging and condemning everyone but themselves. But tell me, what were the points on which you disagreed?"

By-ends answered, "Why, they concluded that it is their duty to rush ahead on their journey in all weather, without waiting for favorable wind or tide. They would risk all in a moment for God, while I, on the other hand, am for taking advantage of all moments to secure my life and my estate. They are for holding their notions, though all other men are against them; but I am for religion so far as the times and my safety will bear it. They are for religion when in rags and contempt; but I am for religion when he walks in his golden slippers in the sunshine and with applause."

Hold-the-world agreed, "Yes, good Mr. By-ends. For my part, I count them fools who lose the things they are at liberty to keep. Let us be wise as serpents; it is best to make hay when the sun shines. You see how the bee lies still all winter and gets busy only when she can have profit along with pleasure.

"God sometimes sends rain and sometimes sunshine. If they are so foolish to go through the first, let us be content to take fair weather along with us. For my part, I like that religion best that will stand with the security of God's good blessings to us.

"Since God has given us the good things of this life, isn't it reasonable to think that He desires that we keep them for His sake? Abraham and Solomon grew rich in religion. And Job says that a good man shall lay up gold as dust. So he must not have had in mind the men who are before us, if they are as you have described them."

"I think that we are all agreed in this matter, and therefore there is no need for any more discussion about it," stated Save-all.

"You are right," Money-love said. "There is nothing more to say about this matter; anyone who does not believe Scripture or reason (and you see we have both on our side) does not know the liberties that he has to seek his own safety and security."

By-ends added, "My friends, we are all on the same pilgrimage. To help pass the time, I would like to propose a question to you: suppose a man—a minister or a tradesman or such—should have an opportunity to get a blessing and improve his station in life by becoming extremely zealous in some point of religion. Let's suppose that this religious point is something about which he has no particular interest, but by appearing to be interested he can gain an advantage, either financial or otherwise. The question I put to you is this: can he pretend to be interested and remain an upstanding, honest man?"

Money-love noted, "I see what your question is getting at, and with these gentlemen's permission I will endeavor to give you an answer. First, I will speak to your question as it concerns a minister. Suppose a minister, a worthy man, but someone with a very small income, has a desire to increase in wealth and influence. Suppose that he sees an opportunity for achieving this goal by becoming more studious, preaching more frequently and zealously, and modifying some of his principles to fit in with the preferences and temperament of his congregation. I see no reason why he cannot do this and a lot more if needed, while still remaining an honest man. And here are the reasons why:

"1. His desire of a greater income is lawful (this cannot be contradicted), since it is set before him by Providence. He should take advantage of the opportunity without questioning his conscience.

"2. Besides, his desire for more income makes him more studious, more zealous in preaching, and so on, and this makes him a better man. Yes, it makes him a better man in all aspects of his life, which also is according to the will of God.

"3. Now, as for his modifying his views and principles to make himself more acceptable to his people, this says three good things about the man. It shows that he is of a self-denying temperament, of a sweet and winning disposition, and thus more fit for ministerial duties.

"4. I conclude, then, that a minister who exchanges a small thing for a great should not be judged as covetous for doing so. Rather, since his decision results in self-improvement and industry, he should be commended as one who pursues his call, and the opportunity should be seen as something that will help him to do good.

"And now to the second part of the question, which concerns the tradesman you mentioned. Suppose this man is in a trade that makes him very little money, but by becoming religious he can improve his income, perhaps get a rich wife, and get better customers to come to his shop. For my part, I see no reason why this may not be lawfully done, and for these reasons:

"1. To become religious is a virtue, by whatever means it happens.

"2. It is not unlawful to marry a rich wife or to encourage a better class of customer to do business in his shop.

"3. Besides, the man who gets these by becoming religious gets something that is good from those who are good by becoming good himself. He gets a good wife, good customers, and a good income, and all by becoming religious, which is good. Therefore, to become religious to get all these is a good and profitable plan."

Mr. Money-love's answer to Mr. By-end's question was highly applauded by them all. They all concluded that it was such a wholesome and advantageous answer that no one would be able to contradict it. And since Christian and Hopeful were still within calling distance, they all agreed to pose these questions and answers to them, since they thought that both of them had been rude in their opposition to Mr. By-ends.

So they called after Christian and Hopeful, who stopped and waited for them to approach. As the three men drew near, they decided that Mr. Hold-the-world, and not Mr. By-ends, should propose the question to Christian and Hopeful to avoid any prejudice that might remain between Mr. By-ends and them.

So they came up to each other, and after a short salutation Mr. Hold-the-world proposed the question to Christian and Hopeful and asked them to answer it if they could.

Then said Christian, "Even a babe in religion could answer ten thousand such questions. For if it is unlawful to follow Christ for loaves, as it says in John 6, how much more abominable is it to make Him and religion into a self-serving device for getting and enjoying the world! Only heathens, hypocrites, devils, and witches are of your opinion.

"The heathens Hamor and Shechem coveted the daughters and cattle of Jacob, and when they saw that there was no way to get them but by becoming circumcised, they said to their companions, 'If every male of us be circumcised, as they are circumcised, will not their cattle and their property and every beast of theirs be ours?' Jacob's daughters and cattle were what the heathen wanted, and they used Jacob's religion as a guise to try to get it. Read the whole story.[b]

---

[b]Genesis 34:20–23.

Christian and Hopeful escape Vanity Fair.

"The hypocritical Pharisees were also of this religion. Long prayers were their pretense, but their intent was to gain the houses and property of widows, and their judgment was greater damnation from God.[c]

"Judas the devil was also of this religion, and he would rather have had the possession of the moneybag than Christ. He was lost, cast away, and the very son of perdition.

"Simon the witch was of this religion also. He wanted the Holy Ghost for the purpose of his own personal financial gain, and you can read in Acts the response of the apostle Peter to his religion.[d]

"It also occurs to me that the man who takes up religion for the world will just as easily throw away religion for the world. For just as Judas desired the world in becoming religious, so did he also sell religion and his Master for the same.

"To answer the question as you have done and to accept your answer as authentic is heathenish, hypocritical, and devilish. You will be rewarded according to your works."

Then they stood staring at one another, unable to answer Christian. Hopeful also approved of the soundness of Christian's answer. So there was a great silence among them.

So Christian and Hopeful continued their journey, but Mr. By-ends and his company stayed behind, stunned by Christian's rebuke.

Then Christian said to Hopeful, "If these men cannot stand before the sentence of men, what will they do before the sentence of God? And if they are mute when dealt with by vessels of clay, what will they do when they shall be rebuked by the flames of a devouring fire?"

---

[c]Luke 20:46–47.
[d]Acts 8:19–20.

Demas invites Christian and Hopeful into the silver mines.

Chapter Nine

REFRESHMENT AT GOD'S RIVER

Then Christian and Hopeful left them again and walked until they came to a smooth plain called Ease, where they traveled with much contentment. The plain was quite small; so they went quickly through it. Now on the far side of that plain was a little hill called Lucre, and in that hill there was a silver mine, which some of the pilgrims had turned aside to see. The ground near the brink of the pit was unstable, and many had stumbled into the pit only to suffer injuries or even death.

Then I saw in my dream that a little off the road, over by the silver mine, stood the gentlemanly Demas calling to passersby to come and see. When he saw Christian and Hopeful he shouted, "Stop! Turn aside, and I will show you something."

"What could be so interesting to see that would turn us out of our way?" Christian asked.

Demas replied, "Over here are men digging in a silver mine for treasure. If you will come and work a little, you may become rich."[1]

Then said Hopeful, "Let's go see."

"Not I," said Christian, "for I have heard of this place and of all the people who have died here digging for treasure. It is a trap that will slow pilgrims down on their journey." Then Christian called to Demas saying, "Is not this place dangerous? Hasn't it hindered many in their pilgrimage?"[a]

"Not very dangerous, except to those who are careless," Demas said, but not without blushing.

Then said Christian to Hopeful, "Let's not miss a step but keep going on our way."

Hopeful said, "I will warrant you that when By-ends comes here, and if he is given the same invitation as we, he will turn out of the way to see."

"I have no doubt you are right, for his principles lead him that way, and the odds are a hundred to one that he dies there," Christian observed.

Then Demas called again, saying, "But will you not come over and see?"

Then Christian sternly answered, saying, "Demas, you are an enemy of the ways of the Lord, and you have already been condemned by one of his Majesty's judges for turning out of the way.[b] Why, then, are you trying to bring us into similar condemnation? Besides, if we turn aside, our Lord the King will certainly hear about it, and we will be put to shame when the time comes when we ought to stand with boldness before Him."

Demas cried out again, saying that he was a brother like them on pilgrimage and that if they would wait for just a little while, he would walk with them.

Then Christian asked, "What is your name? Is it not the same by which I have called you?"

"Yes, my name is Demas. I am the son of Abraham."

Christian asserted, "I know you. Gehazi was your great-grandfather, and Judas was your father, and you have followed in their steps.[c] It is a devilish prank that you use. Your father was hanged as a traitor, and you deserve no better reward. Assure yourself that when we come to the King, we will tell him about

[a]Hosea 4:18.
[b]2 Timothy 4:10.
[c]2 Kings 5:20; Matthew 26:14–15; 27:1–5.

your behavior." Thus said, Christian and Hopeful continued on their way.

By this time By-ends and his companions were again within sight, and at the first invitation they went over to Demas. Now whether they fell into the pit by looking over the brink, or whether they went down to dig, or whether they were smothered in the bottom of the pit by the vapors that came up from the place, I am not certain. But this I do know: they never again were seen along the way of pilgrims.

Then Christian sang:

"By-ends and Silver Demas both agree;
One calls, the other runs, that he may be
A sharer in his lucre; so these do
Take up in this world, and no further go."

Now I saw that just on the other side of the plain, the two pilgrims came to a place in the highway where there stood an old monument. The pilgrims' attention was drawn to the monument because it looked so strange. It seemed to be in the shape of a woman.

As they looked at the statue they were puzzled and could not make sense of it until Hopeful found some strange writing at the head of the pillar. Being no scholar, Hopeful could not understand the meaning of the script. So he called Christian, who was more educated, to see if he could unlock the mystery. Christian spent some time trying to decipher the letters, and finally he understood the inscription's meaning.

Christian then read it aloud to his friend Hopeful: "Remember Lot's wife." They both concluded that the monument rested on the pillar of salt into which Lot's wife was turned after she looked back toward Sodom with a covetous heart.[d2] Seeing this amazing sight gave Christian and Hopeful occasion for the following discourse.

Christian began, "My brother Hopeful, this is a timely sight.

---

[d]Genesis 19:26.

Consider how close this monument is to the Hill of Lucre where Demas gave us the invitation to seek our fortune in the silver mines. If we had done what he enticed us to do, perhaps it would be our statues that other pilgrims would wonder at as they pass this place on the highway."

Hopeful responded, "Yes, and I am sorry that I was so foolish as to even consider it. Only now can I make out the difference between the sin of Lot's wife and my own sin. She only looked back, while I had a desire to go see. Let grace be exalted, and let me be ashamed that such a thought ever entered my heart."

Christian went on, "Let's consider what we have seen here, and let it be a reminder to us in the future. Lot's wife escaped one judgment when she fled the city of Sodom, and yet she was destroyed by another judgment and turned into a pillar of salt."

Hopeful said, "True, and she is a warning and an example to both of us, that we should avoid her sin. She is a visible sign that awaits those who do not take a lesson from this judgment. I am reminded of Korah, Dathan, and Abiram with the 250 men who perished in their sin, who also became a sign or example so that others may take heed.[e] But above all I cannot help thinking about one thing, which is how Demas and his companions can stand so confidently just a little ways from here to look for that treasure for which this woman who simply looked backwards while fleeing the destruction of Sodom was turned into a pillar of salt. It is especially perplexing since the judgment that overtook her made her an example within sight of these men. They cannot help but see her, if they would only lift up their eyes."

"It is bewildering, but it indicates that they have hardened their hearts," Christian continued. "I would compare them to those who pick pockets in the presence of the judge or empty out other people's purses while under the shadow of the gallows. It is said of the men of Sodom that they were exceptional sinners because they were sinners before the Lord. That is to say, they sinned right before His

---

[e]Numbers 26:9–10.

eyes with not enough shame even to try to hide their sin. They did this notwithstanding the kindnesses that He had shown them,[f] for the land of Sodom was like the Garden of Eden.[g] This provoked the Lord, and He made their plague of fire as hot as the Lord of Heaven could make it. The lesson is clear: those who have had examples and warnings put before them and who have received the Lord's benefits and kindness will suffer the most severe judgments if they refuse to repent and change their ways."

Hopeful agreed, "You have spoken the truth, but what a mercy is it that neither you, nor especially I, am made an example! This should give us occasion to thank God, to fear before Him, and to always remember Lot's wife."

Then I saw that they went on their way to a pleasant river that King David called "the river of God" and Saint John called "the river of the water of life."[h] Now since their path lay on the bank of this river, Christian and Hopeful walked with great delight and also drank the water of the river, which was pleasant and enlivening to their weary spirits. On either side of the banks of this river were green trees that produced all kinds of fruit, and the leaves of the trees were good for healing.

Christian and his companion were refreshed as they ate the fruit from the trees. They also ate the leaves and were healed from some of the infirmities that beset travelers in that region.

On either side of the river was a meadow, beautified with lilies and green all the year long. While in this meadow, the two pilgrims lay down and slept, for it was a pleasant and safe place. When they awoke, they gathered the fruit of the trees, drank the water of the river, and then lay down again to sleep.[i] They did this for several days and nights. Then they sang:

> *"Behold ye how these crystal streams do glide,*
> *To comfort pilgrims by the highway side;*

---

[f] Genesis 13:13.
[g] Genesis 13:10.
[h] Psalm 65:9; Revelation 22; see also Ezekiel 47.
[i] Psalm 23:2; Isaiah 14:30.

The meadows green, besides their fragrant smell,
Yield dainties for them: and he that can tell
What pleasant fruit, yea, leaves, these trees do yield,
Will soon sell all, that he may buy this field."

Since they had not yet arrived at their destination, they ate and drank one last time and departed.

Chapter Ten

PRISONERS OF DESPAIR

ow I saw in my dream that they had not journeyed far
before the river parted away from their path. This made
them a little sad, yet they dared not go out of the way.
As their path proceeded away from the river, it became rough,
and their feet were sore from their travels. "So the souls of the
pilgrims were much discouraged because of the way,"[a] and they
wished for a smoother path.

Soon they saw a little way ahead of them a pleasant-looking
field called By-Path Meadow. It sat on the left side of the road, with
a stile marking an entrance into it. Then said Christian to Hopeful,
"If this meadow is right next to the way, let us step aside into it and
walk there." Then they went to the stile to take a look and saw a
path that followed alongside their rough way, just on the other side
of the fence. "This is what I was hoping for," said Christian. "Here
is an easier way to go. Come, good Hopeful, and let us take this
smooth path that follows right next to our difficult one."[1]

"But what if this path should lead us out of the way?" Hopeful
asked.

"That is not likely," said Christian. "Look, doesn't it go right

---

[a]Numbers 21:4.

next to our present path?" So Hopeful, persuaded by Christian, followed after him over the stile into By-Path Meadow.

After they had started walking on the new path, they found it very easy on their feet, and looking ahead, they saw a man walking in the same direction they were going. His name was Vain-Confidence. They called after him and asked him where the path was leading. He yelled back to them, "To the Celestial Gate."

"See," said Christian, "didn't I tell you?"

So they followed Vain-Confidence down the path, but soon the night came, darkness fell, and they lost sight of him. As for Vain-Confidence, who could not see the way ahead of him, he fell into a deep pit[b] that was put there on purpose by the prince of those grounds to catch vainglorious fools. Vain-Confidence was mortally injured when he fell into the pit.

Now Christian and Hopeful heard him fall, so they called up ahead to see if he was all right, but there was no answer except the sound of groaning.

Then Hopeful asked, "Now what should we do?" But Christian was silent, regretting that he had led him out of the way. Then began a torrential rain with fierce thunder and lightning, and the water rose. Then Hopeful groaned in himself, saying, "O that I had kept on the true way!"

"Who could have thought that this path would lead us astray?"

Hopeful continued, "I was afraid it might from the very first, and that is why I gave you that gentle caution. I would have spoken more firmly, but you are older than I."

"Good brother, don't be offended," Christian said soothingly. "I am sorry I have urged you out of the way and that I have put you into such imminent danger. Pray, my brother, forgive me. I did not do it with any evil intent."

Hopeful said warmly, "Be comforted, my brother, I forgive you, and I believe that this will work out for our good."

Christian responded, "I am glad I am traveling with a merciful

---

[b]Isaiah 9:16.

Giant Despair captures Christian and Hopeful.

brother, but we must not stand here. Let's try to get back to where we left the true path."

"But, good brother, let me lead the way."

But Christian offered, "No, if you please, let me go ahead of you so that I can be the first to meet any danger, since I am the one to blame for our present circumstances."

"No," replied Hopeful, "you should not go first. Since your mind is troubled, you might lead us in the wrong direction."

Just then they heard an encouraging voice say, "Set your heart toward the highway, even the way that you went; turn again."[c] But by this time the waters had risen, making it very dangerous to go back the way they had come.

I thought then that it is easier to go out of the way that we are on than to go back onto it when we are off the way.

But despite the risk, they began tracing their steps back to where they had first entered the wrong path. After nearly a dozen near-drownings, and because the darkness made it impossible to see anything, they decided to find a place of shelter where they could wait out the storm until daybreak. After they had found a suitable shelter they soon fell asleep in utter exhaustion.

Not far from the place where they lay sleeping stood a castle called Doubting Castle. The owner of this castle was Giant Despair, and it was on his grounds that they were now sleeping.

When Giant Despair got up in the early morning and began walking up and down in his fields, he came across Christian and Hopeful asleep on his grounds. With a grim and surly voice, he told them to awake and asked them who they were and what they were doing on his property. They told him they were pilgrims and that they had lost their way. Then said the giant, "This night you have trespassed on my property by trampling and lying on my grounds, and therefore you must come along with me." So they were forced to go because he was stronger than they. The pilgrims also had little to say for themselves, knowing that they were at fault.

[c]Jeremiah 31:21.

Giant Despair harasses Christian and Hopeful.

The giant therefore drove them before him and forced them into his castle, where Christian and Hopeful soon found themselves in a dark, nasty, and stinking dungeon.[d] Here they lay from Wednesday morning till Saturday night without one bit of bread or drop of water or ray of light or anyone to inquire about them. So Christian and Hopeful found themselves far from friends and acquaintances, in a hopeless and pitiable condition. Christian had double the sorrow, as he was constantly reminded that it was his ill-advised counsel that had created their present distress.

Giant Despair had a wife whose name was Distrust. When he had gone to bed, he had told his wife that he had taken a couple of prisoners and cast them into his dungeon for trespassing on his grounds. Then he asked her what she thought he should do to them. Distrust inquired about the prisoners' identities, their homeland and destination. He told her they were pilgrims bound for the Celestial City. Then she advised him to beat them without mercy when he arose in the morning.

The next morning when Giant Despair arose, he went out and found a short, thick club made from a crab tree. Then he went down into the dungeon where Christian and Hopeful were imprisoned, and there he began berating them and ranting at them as if they were dogs. Christian and Hopeful did not say a word in their defense.

Then Giant Despair pounced upon them and beat them mercilessly. The beating was so bad that when it was finally over, they were unable to help themselves or even to get up off the dungeon's cold stone floor.

Feeling satisfied with the torment he had inflicted, Giant Despair withdrew, leaving the two prisoners to console each other in their misery and to mourn the rest of the day with the sighs and bitter lamentations of their distress.

The next night, Distrust, discovering that the prisoners were still alive, advised Giant Despair to counsel them to take their own

---

[d]Psalm 88.

lives. So when morning came, the giant went to them in a surly manner as before. Seeing that they were very sore from the previous day's beating, he told them that since they were never likely to come out of that dungeon, their only way of escape would be to make an end of themselves, either with knife, rope, or poison. "For why," said he, "should you choose life, seeing it is attended with so much bitterness?"

But they asked him instead to let them go. Hearing their humble request, he scowled and rushed to make an end of them himself. However, before he could lay hands upon them he fell into one of his fits. It happened occasionally that in sunshiny weather Giant Despair lost for a time the use of his hand. Being thus affected at this time, the giant withdrew and left them to consider their predicament.

Then the prisoners considered whether it was best to take his counsel or not, and this is what they said to each other:

"Brother," said Christian, "what shall we do? The life that we now live is miserable. For my part I do not know which is best: to live like this, or to die and escape this misery. 'My soul chooseth strangling rather than life,' and the grave seems more desirable than this dungeon.[e] Shall we be ruled by the giant?"

Hopeful suggested, "Indeed, our present condition is dreadful, and death would be a relief. But still let us consider that the Lord of the country to which we are going has said, 'You shall do no murder.' And if not to another man, how much more then are we forbidden to take the giant's counsel to kill ourselves? Besides, he who kills another can only commit murder upon a body; but for someone to kill himself is to kill body and soul at the same time. Besides, my brother, you talk about the ease of the grave. But have you forgotten the Hell to which murderers go? For 'no murderer has eternal life.'[f] And let us consider again that the outcome of this is not in the hands of Giant Despair. Other prisoners like us, as far as I can tell,

---

[e]Job 7:15.
[f]1 John 3:15.

who have been captured by the giant, have managed to escape. Who knows but that God, who made the world, may soon cause Giant Despair to die? Or that the giant may forget to lock us in? Or that he may have another one of his fits and lose the use of his limbs? If that ever happens again, I am determined to gather all my courage and try my utmost to escape. I was a fool not to attempt an escape during the first fit. So, my brother, let us be patient and endure for a while longer. The time may come when we have an opportunity to escape, but let's not murder ourselves."

Hopeful's words helped calm Christian's mind, and so they continued together (in the dark) that day in their sad and doleful condition.

That evening the giant went down into the dungeon again to see if his prisoners had taken his counsel, but he found them still alive, though barely. Since the prisoners had had no bread or water and were badly wounded from their beating, they could do little but breathe. Their weak breath was all the sign of life needed to send the giant into a frenzy of rage, and he told them that since they had disobeyed his counsel, it would be worse with them than if they had never been born.

At this they trembled greatly, and Christian fell into a faint. When he recovered, they renewed their discourse about the giant's counsel and whether they should take it or not. Christian seemed inclined toward accepting the giant's advice, but Hopeful was not willing and made his second reply to Christian as follows:

"My brother," he said, "don't you remember how valiant you have been in the past? Apollyon could not crush you, nor were you defeated by all the things you heard, saw, or felt in the Valley of the Shadow of Death. Consider all the hardship, terror, and bewilderment you have already gone through! And now you are full of fear! Don't you see that though I am a far weaker man than you by nature, I inhabit this dungeon with you? The giant has wounded me as well as you and has cut off my bread and water as well as yours. I also mourn without the light. But let us exercise a little more patience. Remember how you conducted yourself in front of the men in Vanity Fair and were afraid neither of the chain, nor the cage, nor even of a bloody death. So let us (at least to avoid this shame that is unbecoming of a Christian) bear this with patience as well as we can."[2]

That same night as Giant Despair went to bed, his wife asked him about the prisoners and if they had taken his counsel. He replied, "They are sturdy rogues, and they would rather endure tremendous hardship than to do away with themselves."

Distrust replied, "Take them into the castle-yard tomorrow, and show them the bones and skulls of those whom you have already killed. Make them believe that before the week's end you will tear them in pieces just as you have done to their fellows before them."

So when the morning came, the giant took his prisoners into the castle-yard and showed them the bones and skulls according to his wife's instructions. "These," said he, "were pilgrims just as you are, and they trespassed on my grounds just as you have done. When I saw fit, I tore them in pieces. I will do the same to you within ten days. Go now, get back down to your den." With that, he beat them all the way down to the dungeon where they lay all day that Saturday in their misery, as they had before.

Now when night had fallen, and when Distrust and her husband had gone to bed, they resumed their conversation about the prisoners. The old giant wondered why he could not by his blows or his counsel bring Christian and Hopeful to an end. His wife replied, "I fear that they live in hope that someone will come to rescue them, or perhaps they have picklocks hidden, by which they hope to escape."

"Do you think so, my dear?" asked the giant. "I will search them in the morning."

Around midnight Christian and Hopeful began to pray and continued till almost the break of day. Shortly before the sun came up, good Christian, as one half-amazed, broke out in this passionate speech: "What a fool I am to lie in a stinking dungeon when I might instead walk at liberty! I have a key in my bosom called Promise that I believe will open any lock in Doubting Castle!"[3]

Hopeful responded, "That is good news, good brother. Take it out, and let's try it."

Then Christian pulled it out of his bosom and began trying to unlock the dungeon door. The door's bolts (as he turned the key) came loose, and the door flew open with ease. Christian and Hopeful both came out. Then Christian went to the outer door that leads into the castle-yard and with his key opened that door also. After that he went to the iron gate, for that also had to be opened. Though that lock was very hard, the key still opened it. Then they thrust open the gate to make a speedy escape, but that gate, as it opened, made a loud creaking noise that awakened Giant Despair. He rose hastily to pursue his prisoners but just then suffered another of his fits, which made his limbs fail and ended his pursuit. Then Christian and Hopeful pressed on eagerly and came to the King's Highway where they were safe because they were out of Giant Despair's jurisdiction.

When they had gone back over the stile, they began to consider what they should do to warn other pilgrims after them who might enter the stile and be taken prisoner by Giant Despair. They agreed to erect a pillar, engraving it with this sentence: "Over this stile is the way to Doubting Castle, which is kept by Giant Despair, who despises the King of the Celestial Country and seeks to destroy His holy pilgrims." Many, therefore, who followed after read what was written and escaped the danger. Having done this, Christian and Hopeful sang as follows:

> *"Out of the way we went, and then we found*
> *What 'twas to tread upon forbidden ground;*
> *And let them that come after have a care,*
> *Lest heedlessness makes them as we to fare.*
> *Lest they for trespassing his prisoners are*
> *Whose castle's Doubting and whose name's Despair."*

Chapter Eleven

SHEPHERDS' WARNINGS, DANGERS AVOIDED

They continued on their path until they came to the Delectable Mountains, which belong to the Lord. Once they arrived, they climbed the mountains to see the gardens, orchards, vineyards, and fountains. From the fountains they drank the water and washed themselves, and they freely ate from the vineyards.[1] Now on the top of these mountains shepherds were feeding their flocks, and they stood by the side of the highway. The pilgrims went to them, and leaning on their staves (as is common with weary pilgrims when they stand to talk), they asked, "Whose Delectable Mountains are these? And whose sheep are these that are pasturing on the mountain?"

A shepherd answered, "These mountains are Immanuel's Land, and they are within sight of His City. The sheep are also His, and He laid down His life for them."[a]

"Is this the way to the Celestial City?" Christian asked.

The shepherd replied, "You are going in the right direction."

"How far is it to get there?" Christian inquired further.

---

[a]John 10:11.

Shepherds comfort Christian and Hopeful.

One of the shepherds said, "Too far for anyone, except those who shall arrive there."

"Is the way safe or dangerous?" Christian wanted to know.

"Safe for those for whom the way is made to be safe, but the transgressors will fall off along the way."[b]

Christian asked, "Is there in this place any relief for pilgrims who are weary and faint in the way?"

A shepherd explained, "The Lord of these mountains has given us a charge not to be 'forgetful to entertain strangers';[c] therefore the benefits of the place are here for you."

I saw also in my dream that when the shepherds perceived that Christian and Hopeful were on pilgrimage, they started asking them questions such as where they had come from and by what means they had entered the way and found strength to persevere. "For few," they said, "who begin the journey make it this far."

When the shepherds heard Christian's and Hopeful's answers, they were pleased and, looking lovingly upon them, warmly welcomed them to the Delectable Mountains.

The shepherds, whose names were Knowledge, Experience, Watchful, and Sincere,[2] took them by the hand and led them to their tents where a meal had been prepared for them. They asked the pilgrims to stay there a while, to get acquainted, and to refresh themselves with all the good things of the Delectable Mountains.[3] Christian and Hopeful told them that they were happy to stay. They then went to rest that night because it was very late.

Then I saw in my dream that in the morning the shepherds called Christian and Hopeful to them and asked them to walk with them upon the mountains. So they went with them and walked a while, having a pleasant view all around them.

Then the shepherds said to one another, "Shall we show these pilgrims some wonders?" So after they had agreed to do it, they took them first to the top of the hill called Error, which was very

---

[b]Hosea 14:9.
[c]Hebrews 13:2.

steep on the far side, and asked them to look down to the bottom. So Christian and Hopeful looked down and saw at the bottom several men dashed to pieces by a fall. Then Christian asked, "What does this mean?"

The shepherds answered, "Haven't you heard of those who fell into error by listening to Hymenaeus and Philetus who denied the faith by refusing to believe in the resurrection of the body?"[d] When they answered that they had, the shepherds continued, "Those whom you see dashed in pieces at the bottom of this mountain are they, and they have continued to this day unburied, as you see, for an example to others to take heed not to clamber too high or come too near the brink of this mountain."

Then I saw that the shepherds took them to the top of another mountain named Caution and asked them look far off. When they did, they saw what they thought were several men walking up and down among the tombs there. They perceived that the men were blind because they stumbled upon the tombs and because they could not get out from among them. Then Christian asked, "What does this mean?"

The shepherds answered, "Do you see a little below these mountains a stile that leads into a meadow on the left hand of this way?" When they spotted it, the shepherds said, "From that stile there is a path that leads directly to Doubting Castle, which is kept by Giant Despair, and these," said the shepherds, pointing to those who were stumbling among the tombs, "were once on pilgrimage just as you are. But when they came to that same stile where the true way was rough, they chose to go out of it into that meadow. Once in the meadow they were taken by Giant Despair and cast into Doubting Castle. After they had been kept in the dungeon for a while, he at last put out their eyes and led them among those tombs where he left them to wander to this very day. The saying of the wise man is fulfilled, 'He that wanders out of the way of understanding shall remain in the congregation of the

---

[d]2 Timothy 2:17–18.

dead.'"[e] Then Christian and Hopeful looked at one another with tears streaming down their faces, but they said nothing to the shepherds.

Then I saw in my dream that the shepherds took them to another place in the bottom of a ravine, where there was a door in the side of the hill. The shepherds opened the door and asked them to look in. They looked and saw that it was very dark and smoky. They also thought they heard a rumbling noise like that of a fire and the cries of someone being tormented, and they smelled the scent of brimstone.

Then Christian asked, "What does this mean?"

The shepherds told them, "This is a byway to Hell, a way that hypocrites enter by doing such things as selling their birthright, like Esau, or selling their master, like Judas, or blaspheming the gospel, like Alexander, or lying and dissembling, like Ananias and Sapphira, his wife."

Then said Hopeful to the shepherds, "I perceive that all of these people you have mentioned had the appearance of being pilgrims, just as we do, did they not?"

"Yes, and for a long time too," a shepherd replied.

Hopeful inquired, "How long did they appear to go on their pilgrimage before they were miserably cast away?"

A shepherd answered, "Some came as far as these mountains, some even farther, and some were lost long before they ever got here."

Then the pilgrims said to one another, "We need to cry to the Strong One for strength."

"Yes," a shepherd agreed, "and you will have need to use that strength when you get it."

By this time all agreed that the pilgrims should continue their journey, so they walked together toward the end of the mountains. Then the shepherds said to one another, "Let us show the pilgrims the gates of the Celestial City, if they have skill to look through

---

[e]Proverbs 21:16.

our telescope." The pilgrims consented eagerly to the idea. So they took them to the top of a high hill called Clear and gave them their telescope, which the pilgrims carefully looked through. But their recollections of all that the shepherds had just shown them made them tremble a little, causing their hands to shake and making it difficult to see clearly through the glass. But they thought they saw something like a gate and also some of the glory of the place. As they prepared to depart these mountains, they sang this song:

> *"Thus by the shepherds secrets are revealed,*
> *Which from all other men are kept concealed.*
> *Come to the shepherds, then, if you would see*
> *Things deep, things hid, and that mysterious be."*

Before they departed, the shepherd Knowledge gave them a map of the way. Another shepherd, Experience, told them to beware of the Flatterer. The third, Watchful, warned them not to sleep on the Enchanted Ground. And the fourth, Sincere, bid them Godspeed. So I awoke from my dream.[4]

Christian and Hopeful gaze at the Celestial City.

Chapter Twelve

Faith under Attack

I slept again, and I dreamed I saw the same two pilgrims going down the mountains along the highway toward the Celestial City. Now a little below these mountains on the left-hand side lies the country of Conceit.[1] From this country meandered a twisting but pleasant green lane that joined the pilgrims' highway. It was here that Christian and Hopeful met a very brisk lad who was coming out of that country. His name was Ignorance. Christian asked him where he came from and where he was going.

"Sir, I was born in the country that lies off to the left, and I am going to the Celestial City."

Christian asked, "But how do you think you will enter in at the Celestial Gate? I think you may find some difficulty there."

"As other good people do," said he.

Christian asked again, "But what have you to show at the gate that will cause it to be opened to you?"

"I know my Lord's will, and I have lived a good life," Ignorance said confidently. "I pay every man what I owe him; I pray and fast; I pay tithes and give alms; and I have left my country to go to the Celestial City."[2]

Christian challenged, "But you did not enter at the narrow

sheep gate at the beginning of this way. Instead, you have come into the way through a crooked lane. Therefore, I am afraid that whatever you think of yourself, you will be accused of being a thief and a robber on the day of reckoning, gaining no admittance to the Celestial City."

"Gentlemen, you are complete strangers to me. I do not know you," Ignorance stated. "Be content to follow the religion of your country, and I will follow the religion of mine. I hope that all will be well. And as for the narrow sheep gate that you talk of, the entire world knows that it is far away from our country. I cannot imagine that anyone in these parts even knows how to find it, nor do they need to bother since, as you can see, we have a fine, pleasant, green lane that comes down from our country and joins the way directly."

When Christian saw that the man was "wise in his own conceit," he said to Hopeful, whisperingly, "'There is more hope for a fool than for him.'"[a] And he also said, "'When he that is a fool walketh by the way, his wisdom faileth him, and he saith to everyone that he is a fool.'[b] What do you think?" continued Christian. "Should we continue walking with him, or should we walk away from him and give him time to think about what we have told him? We could stop and wait for him later and see if by degrees we can do him any good."

Then said Hopeful:

> *"Let Ignorance a little while now muse*
> *On what is said, and let him not refuse*
> *Good counsel to embrace, lest he remain*
> *Still ignorant of what's the chiefest gain.*
> *God saith, those that no understanding have*
> *(Although He made them), them He will not save."*

He further added, "I do not think it is a good idea to tell him everything at once. Let's pass him by for now, and if you would like, we will talk to him later. Perhaps he will be better able to consider what we've told him if he is given some time to do so."[3]

---

[a]Proverbs 26:12.
[b]Ecclesiastes 10:3.

So Christian and Hopeful both went on ahead, and Ignorance remained behind them. After a little while they entered into a dark lane where they saw a man whom seven demons had bound with seven strong cords. The demons were carrying him back to the door that Christian and Hopeful had seen with the shepherds on the side of the hill.[c]

Now good Christian and Hopeful began to tremble as the devils led the man away. Christian looked to see if he knew the man who was bound, and he thought he recognized him as one Turn-Away who lived in the town of Apostasy.[4] But he could not clearly see his face, for the bound man hung his head like a captured thief. Once they had passed, Hopeful looked after him and saw on his back a paper with the inscription, "Wanton professor and damnable apostate."[5]

Then said Christian to his friend Hopeful, "Now I remember something I was told about a good man who once lived in these parts. The name of the man was Little-Faith.[6] He was a good man, and he lived in the town of Sincere. The story I was told was as follows:

"Upon a part of this highway near us, Little-Faith encountered a road called Dead Man's Lane, which joins the highway from Broad-Way Gate. It is called Dead Man's Lane because of all the murders that are commonly done there. This man Little-Faith, who was going on his pilgrimage just as we are now, happened to sit down and fall asleep close by this dangerous lane. Now it just so happened that around the same time, three sturdy rogues named Faint-Heart, Mistrust, and Guilt (three brothers) were coming down the lane from Broad-Way Gate. They saw Little-Faith and came galloping up to him at full speed just as Little-Faith was awakening from his sleep and was preparing to continue his journey. Being taken thus by surprise, Little-Faith was powerless to run and, being outnumbered, was powerless to fight. The rogues demanded with threatening language that he stand up and hand over his wallet and money. White as a cloud with fear, Little-Faith

[c]Matthew 12:45; Proverbs 5:22.

stood up but was slow to hand over his money, reluctant to part with it. So Mistrust ran up to him, thrust his hand into his pocket, and pulled out a bag of silver.

Then Little-Faith cried out, "Thieves! Thieves!" But Guilt struck Little-Faith on the head with a club, knocking him flat to the ground where he lay bleeding profusely.[7] Heedless of the wounded man, the thieves just stood by, counting the stolen silver. But finally they heard someone approaching on the road, and fearing it might be Great-Grace who dwells in the city of Good Confidence, they ran off and left Little-Faith to tend to himself. After a while, Little-Faith came to and, gathering what strength he had left, got up and tended his wound as best he could and hobbled on his way.[8] This was the story I was told."

"Did the three thieves steal everything he had?" Hopeful asked.

Christian reported, "No, they did not find his jewels that he had hidden. But as I said, the good man suffered for his loss, since the thieves stole most of his spending money. And even though they did not find his jewels, he was still left with barely enough money to finish his journey.[d] Unless I am misinformed, he was forced to beg for enough food to sustain himself as he went on the rest of his pilgrimage. He did not sell his jewels, so he was left to beg and do what he could as he went on his way. I am told that he was hungry and malnourished for most of the rest of his journey."[9]

"Isn't it amazing that the thieves did not steal his certificate by which he was to receive his admittance at the Celestial Gate?" Hopeful wondered.

Christian commented, "It is a wonder that they missed it, although it was not through any cunning on the part of Little-Faith. He was caught off guard by them and had neither the power nor the skill to hide anything from them. It was more by God's gracious providence than by Little-Faith's own endeavors that they missed his certificate."[e]

----

[d] 1 Peter 4:18.
[e] 2 Timothy 1:14; 2 Peter 2:9.

Hopeful added, "But it must have been a comfort to him that they did not get this particular jewel, this certificate, from him."

"It might have been great comfort to him if he had used it as he should; but those who told me the story said that he made little use of this treasure for all the rest of the journey. I was told that because of the trauma he experienced at the hands of the thieves, he seemed to almost forget that he possessed the certificate. On the few occasions when he remembered it and might have been relieved by the thought of still having it, the memory of his loss would rush upon him and swallow up all hope and reason."

"Alas! Poor man!" Hopeful exclaimed. "This must have been a great grief to him."

Christian echoed, "Yes, grief indeed. What if we had been robbed and wounded while traveling in a strange place? It is a wonder he did not die with grief, poor heart! I was told that he spent almost all the rest of the way bitterly complaining, telling everyone he met on the way about every detail of how he was robbed, wounded, and left for dead."

Hopeful continued, "But what surprises me is that in his desperate situation he did not sell or pawn some of his hidden jewels, which may have given him some relief on his journey."

"What, do you really mean this?" Christian challenged. "Then you don't see the full picture, like a newborn bird with its shell still on its head. For what should he pawn them, or to whom should he sell them? In the country where he was robbed, his jewels were not considered valuable. Nor did he seek the kind of relief that anyone of that country could give. Besides, had his jewels been missing at the gate of the Celestial City, he would have been excluded from his inheritance (a fact of which he was well aware). Had he parted with his jewels, he would have been in worse shape than if he had been attacked by ten thousand thieves."

"Why are you so harsh, my brother?" Hopeful protested. "Esau sold his birthright for a mess of pottage, and that birthright was his greatest jewel; and if Esau could sell his jewel, then why couldn't Little-Faith do the same?"[f]

Christian asserted, "Esau did sell his birthright indeed, and so do many others, and by so doing exclude themselves from the chief blessing. But you must understand the difference between Esau and Little-Faith and also the difference between their estates. Esau's birthright was the shadow, but Little-Faith's jewels were the substance. Esau's belly was his god, but Little-Faith's belly was not. Esau's interests were in his fleshly appetite, but Little-Faith's were not. Esau could see no further than the fulfilling of his lusts. 'Behold, I am at the point to die (he said), and what profit shall this birthright do me?'[g] But Little-Faith, though it was his lot to have only a small portion of faith, was made to see and prize his jewels by faith and not to sell them, as Esau did his birthright. You do not read anywhere that Esau had faith, not even a little. So it is not a surprise that a man who is ruled by his fleshly passions and appetites is willing to sell his birthright and his soul to the Devil who resides in Hell. He is like the donkey that stubbornly goes in the wrong direction.[h] When such persons' minds are set upon their lusts, they will have them whatever the cost.

"But Little-Faith was of another temperament. His mind was fixed on things divine; his interests were upon things that were spiritual and from above. What would be the purpose for someone of Little-Faith's character to sell his spiritual treasure (had there been any who would have bought them) in order to possess the empty things of this world? Will a man pay to fill his belly with hay? Or can you persuade the turtledove to live upon carrion like the crow? Faithless ones can sell, pawn, or mortgage what they have, and themselves in the bargain, for carnal lusts; but those who have faith, saving faith, even though it is little, cannot do so. That is where you made your mistake, my brother."

---

[f]Hebrews 12:16.
[g]Genesis 25:32.
[h]Jeremiah 2:24.

Hopeful stated, "I acknowledge my mistake, but your abrupt response nearly made me angry."

Christian explained, "Why, I simply compared you to some newly hatched birds of a brisker variety that will run without thinking to and fro in unfamiliar paths, with part of their remaining shell still upon their heads. But get over that and consider the matter under debate, and all shall be well between you and me."[10]

Hopeful went on, "I am persuaded that these three fellows who attacked Little-Faith are a company of cowards. Why else would they have run when they heard the noise of someone coming down the road? Why then did Little-Faith lack courage? He might have stood his ground against them and yielded only after exhausting all other remedies."

Christian suggested, "Many have said that the three thieves were cowards, but few in the time of trial have withstood them courageously. As far as more courage, Little-Faith had none to spare. I understand that you recommend a brief brush with the rogues before yielding. This is your recommendation when they are far away from us, but I wonder if you would not have second thoughts if they were to come rushing unexpectedly on you? Also consider that they are journeymen thieves and that they serve under the king of the bottomless pit. If they called on him, he would come immediately to their aid, and he has a voice like a roaring lion.[i]

"I have been in a situation similar to that of Little-faith, and I found it a terrible thing. These three villains once attacked me, and like a courageous Christian, I resisted at first. Then they called to their master who joined them in the attack. I would, as the saying goes, have given my life for a penny, but as God would have it, I was clothed with proven armor that protected me, yet also made it difficult to stand up and fight like a man. No one can know the risks and hazards of a battle unless he has been in the battle himself."

"Yes," Hopeful somewhat agreed, "but they still seem to me to

---

[i] Psalm 7:2; 1 Peter 5:8.

be cowards, for they ran away when they thought Great-Grace was on the way."

"True, they have often fled, both they and their master, when Great-Grace has appeared," Christian acknowledged. "That is not a surprise, for he is the King's Champion. I think you must make a distinction between Little-Faith and the King's Champion. Not all the King's subjects are His champions, nor can they all do such feats of war as a champion. Do you think that a little child could handle Goliath as David did? Or does a wren possess the strength of an ox? Some are strong, some are weak; some have great faith, some have little. This man was one of the weak, and therefore he was overcome by the thieves' evil designs."

Hopeful said, "I wish it had been Great-Grace whom the thieves had met."

"If it had been, he might have had his hands full with the three of them," Christian asserted. "Even though Great-Grace is excellent with his weapons, he does well only when he can keep them at the end of his sword point. But if Faint-Heart or Mistrust or Guilt should get close to him and knock him down, what then? If you look upon Great-Grace's face, you will see scars and cuts there that demonstrate what I have been saying. I have heard that he has despaired even of life when in combat. Didn't these same sturdy rogues and their companions make David groan, moan, and roar? Heman and Hezekiah, who were champions in their day, were severely tested when assaulted by these same rogues. Peter, who some say is the prince of the apostles, was so put to the test that by the time they were through with him he was afraid of a servant girl. And remember, these villains' king is at their beck and call. He is never out of earshot; and whenever they begin to have a difficult time, he comes in to help them if he can.

"But as for footmen like you and me, let us never desire to meet with the enemy or presume ourselves able to do better when we hear about the struggles of others. When we hear of others who have been sorely tested, let's not be deluded by thoughts of our own manhood, for those who do so are often the ones who have the worst time of it when they are tested.

"Witness Peter, of whom I made mention before. He would swagger indeed, and his vain mind prompted him to say that he would stand up for his Master when all others fled for fear. But who was it who fled in fear when these villains arrived on the scene? When we hear that such robberies are done on the King's Highway, there are two things we should do:

"1. To go out armed, being sure to take our shield with us. The Devil has no fear of us at all if he finds us without our shield. Remember what we learned? 'Above all, taking the shield of faith, wherewith ye shall be able to quench all the fiery darts of the wicked.'[j]

"2. It is also a good idea to travel in a convoy and request that the Lord go with us Himself. This made David rejoice when he was in the Valley of the Shadow of Death, and Moses would rather have died where he stood than to go one step without his God.[k] O my brother, if He will go along with us, then we need not fear even if tens of thousands set themselves against us.[l] But without Him the proud pilgrims 'fall among the slain.'[m]

"As for my part, I have been in the battle before, and I cannot boast of my own strength or courage. I stand before you alive because of the grace and goodness of my Lord. I would be very glad to never go through another such time of testing and danger. However, since the lion and the bear have not as yet devoured me, I hope God will also deliver us from the next uncircumcised Philistine."

Then sang Christian:

"Poor Little–Faith! Have you been among the thieves?
Were you robbed? Remember this, whosoever believes
And gets more faith shall then a victor be
Over ten thousand, else scarce over three."

---

[j]Ephesians 6:16.
[k]Exodus 33:15.
[l]Psalm 3:5–8; 27:1–3.
[m]Isaiah 10:4.

So Christian and Hopeful continued on their journey, with Ignorance following behind them. They continued on until they came to a place where there was a fork in the road. As they looked down each path, both appeared to be as straight as the other. They did not know which way to go.

Chapter Thirteen

FLATTERING ENEMIES AND
RENEWED TRUST

s they were deciding which of the two paths to take, a man of dark complexion, covered by a white robe, came to them and asked with a very pleasant demeanor why they were standing there. They answered that they were going to the Celestial City but did not know which of the paths to take. "Follow me," encouraged the man agreeably, "for that is where I am going."[1]

So they followed him, and the way he took them turned by degrees until they were walking in a direction away from the Celestial City. Despite this bend in the road, the pilgrims were not alarmed and continued to follow the man.[2]

But by and by, before they were aware of it, he had led them both within the range of a net in which they were suddenly so entangled that they knew not what to do. With that the white robe fell off the dark man's back. Then they saw that they had been led into a trap, and there they lay weeping for some time, for they could not get themselves untangled from the net.[3]

Then Christian said to Hopeful, "Now I see my error. Didn't the shepherds tell us to beware of the Flatterers? We have discovered for ourselves the meaning of the wise man's saying, 'A man that flattereth his neighbor spreadeth a net for his feet.'"[a]

Hopeful reminded him, "They also gave us a map so we could avoid the paths of the Destroyer, but we forgot to look at it. On this matter David was indeed wiser than we, for he said, 'Concerning the works of men, by the word of Thy lips I have kept myself from the paths of the destroyer.'"[b]

While they lay hopelessly tangled in the net, chiding themselves for their error, they saw a Shining One coming toward them. He had a whip of small cords in his hand.

When he had come up to them, he asked them where they came from and what they were doing there. They told him that they were poor pilgrims going to Zion but had been led out of their way by a dark, deceptive man clothed in white who had asked them to follow him, pretending to be a pilgrim bound for Zion.

Then the Shining One with the whip said, "It is the Flatterer, a false apostle who has transformed himself into an angel of light."[c] So he tore open the net and let them out. Then he said to them, "Follow me, and I will take you back to the right way." So he led them back to the way that they had left to follow the Flatterer.

Then he asked them, "Where did you spend last night?" They said that they had been sheltered by the shepherds on the Delectable Mountains. He then asked them if the shepherds had given them a map with directions, which they affirmed. The Shining One continued, "When you came to the other path that crossed the way, did you take out your map and read the directions?" When they admitted that they hadn't because they had forgotten, the Shining One asked them if the shepherds had warned them to beware of the Flatterer.

"Yes," they answered, "but we did not imagine that this fine-spoken man was he."[d]

Then I saw in my dream that he commanded them to lie down.

---

[a]Proverbs 29:5.
[b]Psalm 17:4.
[c]Daniel 11:32; 2 Corinthians 11:13–14.
[d]Romans 16:18.

When they did, he chastised them with his whip till they were sore in order to teach them to walk only in the good way.[e] As he chastised them, he said, "As many as I love, I rebuke and chasten; be zealous, therefore, and repent."[f] After this he sent them back on their way with instructions to pay attention to the map and the directions given to them by the shepherds. So they thanked him for all his kindness and went meekly along the right way, singing:

> "Come hither, you that walk along the way;
> See how the pilgrims fare that go astray!
> They are caught in an entangling net,
> 'Cause they good counsel lightly did forget:
> 'Tis true, they were rescued, but yet you see,
> They're scourged to boot. Let this your caution be."

Now after a while, they saw a man afar off coming toward them. He was traveling alone. Then Christian said to Hopeful, "Look, a man with his back toward Zion is coming to meet us."

"I see him," Hopeful said. "Let us be careful that he is not another Flatterer."

So he drew nearer and at last met up with them. His name was Atheist, and he asked them where they were going.

"We are going to Mount Zion," Christian announced.

At this answer Atheist began to laugh uncontrollably.[4]

"Why are you laughing?" inquired Christian.

Atheist answered, "I am laughing at how ignorant you are to endure such a tedious journey and get nothing for your trouble but all the pain that goes along with such a journey."

"Why, do you think we won't be received at the Celestial City?" Christian asked.

"Received where?" Atheist asked in turn. "There is no such place as the Celestial City in all this world!"[5]

"But there is in the world to come."

Atheist continued, "When I was at home in my own country, I

[e]Deuteronomy 25:2; 2 Chronicles 6:26–27.
[f]Revelation 3:19.

heard about the Celestial City and went to find it for myself. I have spent the last twenty years seeking this city and am not any closer to finding it than the day I began looking for it."[g]

"We have both heard and believed that there is such a place to be found," Christian remarked.

Atheist asserted, "If I had not believed it existed, I would not have spent all this time looking for it. Having spent more time looking for it than you have, I can certainly assure you that the place does not exist, and so it cannot be found. I am now on my way back to get my share of those pleasures I denied myself in my useless journey to find something that does not exist."[6]

Then Christian asked Hopeful, "Is this man speaking truthfully?"

Hopeful warned, "Take heed; he is one of the Flatterers. Remember what it has cost us once already for listening to men such as this. What, no Mount Zion? Didn't we see the gates of the Celestial City from the Delectable Mountains? Also, aren't we in this present time to walk by faith?[h] Let's go on," said Hopeful. "If we do not continue on our way, the man with the whip may overtake us again. You should be the one teaching me the lesson that I will now say to you: 'Cease, my son, to hear the instruction that causeth to err from the words of knowledge.'[i] I say, my brother, cease to hear him, and let us 'believe to the saving of the soul.'"[j]

Christian explained, "My brother, I did not put the question to you because I doubted the truth, but to test you and to pull out of your own heart an honest expression of your faith. As for this man, I know that he is blinded by the god of this world.[k] Let us go on, knowing that we have believed the truth, 'and no lie is of the truth.'"[l]

"Now I rejoice in the hope of the glory of God,"[m] Hopeful said.

[g]Jeremiah 22:13; Ecclesiastes 10:15.
[h]2 Corinthians 5:7.
[i]Proverbs 19:27.
[j]Hebrews 10:39.
[k]1 John 2:11.
[l]1 John 2:21.
[m]Romans 5:2.

So they turned away from the man, who laughed and went on his way.[7]

Then I saw in my dream that they continued their journey until they came into a region where the air naturally induced sleepiness if one was not acclimated to it. Here Hopeful began to grow very sluggish and sleepy. He said to Christian, "I am starting to grow drowsy and can scarcely keep my eyes open. Let's lie down and take a nap."

"By no means," said Christian. "We might fall asleep and never wake up."

"Why so, my brother?" Hopeful asked. "Sleep is sweet for the travel-weary man, and a little nap would be refreshing."

"Do you recall that one of the shepherds told us to beware of the Enchanted Ground?" Christian inquired. "He meant that we should beware of sleeping. 'Therefore let us not sleep, as do others, but let us watch and be sober.'"[n][8]

Hopeful agreed, "You're right, and had I been here alone I would be asleep by now and in danger of death. What the wise man says is true, 'Two are better than one.'[o] Your company has been God's mercy to me, and 'you shall have a good reward for your labor.'"[p]

"Now then," said Christian, "to prevent us from becoming drowsy in this place, perhaps we should have a good discussion."[9]

"I wholeheartedly agree," said Hopeful.

"Where shall we begin?"

"Where God began with us,"[10] Hopeful suggested. "But you begin, if you please."

Christian said, "First I will sing you this song:

"When saints do sleepy grow, let them come hither
And hear how these two pilgrims talk together.
Yea, let them learn of them, in any wise,
Thus to keep open their drowsy slumbering eyes.
Saints' fellowship, if it be managed well,
Keeps them awake, and that in spite of Hell."

---

[n] 1 Thessalonians 5:6.
[o] Ecclesiastes 4:9.
[p] Ecclesiastes 4:9.

Then Christian began, saying, "I will ask you a question. What made you decide to begin this journey?"

"Do you mean to ask how I first become concerned about the condition of my soul?" Hopeful questioned.

"Yes, that is what I mean."

Hopeful began, "For a very long time I was delighted with all the things you could see and buy at Vanity Fair. I am certain that had I continued in this way I would have been drowned in perdition and destruction."

"What kinds of things are you talking about?" Christian wondered.

"All the treasures and riches of the world," Hopeful said. "Also I delighted in rioting, reveling, drinking, swearing, lying, uncleanness, Sabbath-breaking, and all the other things that destroy the soul. But one day I began to hear and consider things that are divine, which I heard from you and the beloved Faithful, who was put to death for his faith and the testimony of his good life in Vanity Fair. I was convicted that 'the end of these things is death'q and that for these things' sake 'cometh the wrath of God upon the children of disobedience.'"r

"And did you immediately come under the power of this conviction?" Christian questioned further.

Hopeful acknowledged, "No, I was not immediately willing to acknowledge the evil of sin or the damnation that follows sinning. When my mind began to be stirred up by the Word, I tried to shut my eyes to the truth of it."

"What kept you from understanding that God was working through His blessed Spirit to bring you to Himself?"

Hopeful explained, "The reasons were as follows. First of all, I was ignorant that this was the work of God in my life, since I never imagined that God begins His work of conversion in a sinner's life by awakening him to his sin. Then there was the appeal that sin

---

qRomans 6:21–23.
rEphesians 5:6.

still held over my flesh, and I was reluctant to abandon it. Another reason I refused then to repent is that I did not want to part ways with my old companions whose company and entertainments were very desirable to me. Finally, the times in which I came under the conviction of sin were so troublesome and frightening that I did everything I could to try to cast these times out of my memory."

"Then there were times when you were not troubled in your mind and soul?" Christian queried.

"Yes," Hopeful said, "that is true, but it would creep back into my mind, and then my soul would be as troubled as it was before, or even worse."

"What was it that brought your sins to mind again?"

Hopeful answered, "Many things, such as the following:

"1. If I met a good man in the streets; or,

"2. If I heard the Bible being read; or,

"3. If my head ached; or,

"4. If I was told that some of my neighbors were sick; or,

"5. If I heard the bell toll for the dead; or,

"6. If I thought of dying myself; or,

"7. If I heard about someone's sudden death,

"8. And lastly, the thing that brought my sin to mind and troubled my soul worse than all of these things was when I thought to myself that I must quickly come to judgment."

"And when these things reminded you of your sin," Christian stated, "could you find relief from the sense of guilt that your sin caused?"

"No, I could not," Hopeful said. "If I even thought about returning to one of my previous sins, my conscience would torment me."

"And then what did you think?" Christian asked.

Hopeful went on, "I thought about changing my ways, afraid that if I did not, I would be damned."

"And did you try to change your ways?"

Hopeful answered, "Yes. Not only did I flee from my sin, but from sinful company also; and I took up religious duties such as prayer, Bible reading, weeping for my sin, speaking the truth to my neighbors, and so on. I did all these things and many others too numerous to relate."

"And did this give you peace of mind?" Christian inquired.

"Yes, for a while," Hopeful reported. "But in the end my trouble came tumbling back upon me again, despite all my reformations."

"How did that come about since you were now reformed?" Christian wondered.

Hopeful continued, "Several things brought it about. I began to read in my Bible where it said things like 'All our righteousness is as filthy rags'[s] and 'By the works of the law shall no flesh be justified'[t] and 'When ye shall have done all those things, say, "We are unprofitable"'[u] and many other such sayings. Then I began to reason with myself: If all my righteousness is as filthy rags, if by the deeds of the Law no man can be justified, and if when we have done all we can do, we remain still unprofitable, then it is folly to think that I will enter Heaven by keeping the Law. It also occurred to me that if a man runs a hundred pounds into debt with a shopkeeper and then begins to pay cash for everything else he purchases, while leaving the old debt unpaid, the shopkeeper can rightfully sue him and cast him into prison until he pays all his past debt."

"Well, how did you apply this to yourself?" Christian asked further.

Hopeful explained, "Why, I thought about how great a debt of sin I had run up in God's book and how even if I reformed myself, I could not pay off this past debt. So how could I be freed from the damnation that I have brought upon myself by my former transgressions?"

Christian affirmed, "A very good application, but go on."

Hopeful added, "Another thing that troubled me is that when I carefully looked into my new best efforts, I saw that they were

---

[s] Isaiah 64:6.
[t] Galatians 2:16.
[u] Luke 17:10.

mixed up with sin. I was forced to conclude that even if I could conceivably ignore all past sins, including the sin of pride and conceit I had in myself because of my former 'good' deeds, I have committed enough sin in one of my most recent good duties to send me to Hell, even if my former life had been somehow found faultless."

"And what did you do then?" Christian asked.

"Do!" Hopeful exclaimed. "I couldn't figure out what to do until I shared my concerns with Faithful, for he and I were well acquainted. He told me that unless I could obtain the righteousness of a Man who never had sinned, neither my own righteousness nor all the righteousness of the world could save me."

"And did you think he spoke the truth?" Christian questioned.

Hopeful answered, "Had he told me this when I was pleased and satisfied with my reformed life, I would have called him a fool for his pains. But since I was now aware of my own weakness and the sin that cleaves to my best performance, I was forced to believe his opinion."

"But did you think, when he suggested it to you, that there was a Man of whom it might justly be said that He never committed sin?" Christian offered.

Hopeful said, "I must confess that the words sounded strange at first, but after keeping company and talking with Faithful, I fully believed that there was such a Man."

"And did you ask him who this Man was and how you could be justified by Him?" Christian queried.

"Yes," Hopeful replied, "and he told me it was the Lord Jesus, who sits on the right hand of the Most High. And he told me that I could be justified by Him if I would trust in what He Himself had done in the days when He lived on earth, when He suffered and hung on the tree. I asked him how that Man's righteousness could be effective to justify another before God. Faithful replied that Jesus was the mighty God, having done what He did and dying the shameful death not for Himself but for me who deserved it instead.

If I would believe in Him and what He had done for me, then His worthiness would be imputed to me."[v]

"What did you do then?"

Hopeful said, "I objected to his argument because I thought that Man was not willing to save me."

"So how did Faithful reply to that?" Christian questioned.

Hopeful recounted, "He told me to go to Him and see for myself. Then I objected that it would be presumptuous; but he said it would not be, for I had been invited to come.[w] Then he gave me the Book of Jesus to encourage me more freely to come. Faithful told me that the words in this book, including the smallest detail, stood firmer than Heaven and earth.[x]

"Then I asked him, 'What must I do when I come to Him?' He answered that I must plead upon my knees, with all my heart and soul, that the Father reveal Him to me.[y] Then I asked him further how I must make my supplication to Him. And he said that if I go to Him I would find Him upon a mercy-seat, where He sits all the year long to give pardon and forgiveness to all those who come.

"I told him that I didn't know what to say when I came. Then Faithful told me to say words to this effect: 'God, be merciful to me a sinner, and make me to know and believe in Jesus Christ. For I see that if His righteousness had not been offered, or if I have no faith in that righteousness, I am utterly cast away. Lord, I have heard that You are a merciful God and have ordained that Your Son Jesus Christ should be the Savior of the world. Moreover, You are willing to give Him for a poor sinner like me (and I am a sinner indeed). Lord, take therefore this opportunity, and magnify Your grace in the salvation of my soul, through Your Son Jesus Christ. Amen.'"[z]

"So did you do as you were asked?" Christian wondered.

"Yes," Hopeful replied, "right then and many times over."

---

[v]Hebrews 10; Romans 4; Colossians 1; 1 Peter 1.
[w]Matthew 11:28.
[x]Matthew 24:35.
[y]Psalm 95:6; Daniel 6:10; Jeremiah 29:12–13.
[z]Exodus 25:22; Leviticus 16:2; Numbers 7:89; Hebrews 4:16.

"And did the Father reveal His Son to you?" Christian inquired further.

"Neither at the first, nor second, nor third, nor fourth, nor fifth, no, nor at the sixth time," Hopeful answered honestly.

Christian asked, "What did you do then?"

Hopeful responded, "Why, I didn't know what to do."

"Did you think that you might stop praying?" Christian asked softly.

"Yes, a hundred times," Hopeful confessed.

"And what was the reason you did not?" Christian questioned.

Hopeful told him, "I believed that what Faithful told me was true and that without the righteousness of this Christ, all the world could not save me. Therefore, I thought to myself, if I stop praying I will die, and I only wish to die at the throne of grace. And with these words came into my mind, 'Though it tarry, wait for it; because it will surely come, it will not tarry.'[aa] So I continued praying until the Father showed me His Son."

"And how was He revealed to you?" Christian asked.

Hopeful explained, "I did not see Him with my bodily eyes, but with the eyes of my understanding,[ab] and it happened like this: One day I was very sad, probably sadder than ever before, and this sadness resulted from a fresh glimpse of the great depth and vileness of my sins. I was expecting nothing but Hell and the everlasting damnation of my soul. Suddenly I saw the Lord Jesus look down from Heaven upon me and say, 'Believe on the Lord Jesus Christ, and you will be saved.'[ac]

"'But,' I replied, 'Lord, I am a great, a very great, sinner.'

"He answered, 'My grace is sufficient for you.'[ad]

"Then I said, 'But, Lord, what is believing?'

"Then I understood from the Scripture that believing and coming were the same thing: 'He that cometh to Me shall never hunger,

---

[aa]Habakkuk 2:3.
[ab]Ephesians 1:18–19.
[ac]Acts 16:31.
[ad]2 Corinthians 12:9.

and he that believeth on Me shall never thirst.'ae Thus, those who have come to Jesus, who have run wholeheartedly to Christ for salvation, have indeed believed in Christ. Then I wept, and I asked again, 'But, Lord, will You indeed accept and save even such a great sinner as I?'

"And I heard Him say, 'He that cometh to Me, I will in no wise cast out.'af

"Then I asked, 'But how can I know that my faith is truly placed upon You?'

"Then He said, 'Christ Jesus came into the world to save sinners.'ag 'He is the end of the law for righteousness to every one who believes.'ah 'He died for our sins, and rose again for our justification.'ai 'He loved us and washed us from our sins in His own blood.'aj 'He is mediator between God and man.'ak 'He ever lives to make intercession for us."al

"From all this I understood that I must look for righteousness in His person and for satisfaction for my sins by His blood. I must believe that what He did in obedience to His Father's law, in submitting to the penalty for sin, was not for Himself but for him who will accept it for his salvation and be thankful. Finally my heart was full of joy, my eyes full of tears, and my affections running over with love for the name, people, and ways of Jesus Christ."

"This was a revelation of Christ to your soul indeed," Christian confirmed. "But tell me also what particular effect this had upon your spirit."

Hopeful said, "It made me consider that this world, notwithstanding all the good things and noble deeds in it, is in a state of condemnation. It made me see that God the Father, though He is perfectly just and thus must punish all sin, can rightly justify the

---

aeJohn 6:35.
afJohn 6:37.
ag1 Timothy 1:15.
ahRomans 10:4.
aiRomans 4:25.
ajRevelation 1:5.
ak1 Timothy 2:5.
alHebrews 7:25.

sinner who comes to Him in His Son. It made me greatly ashamed of the vileness of my former life and confounded me with the sense of my own ignorance, for until that moment I had never once been filled with thoughts of the beauty of Jesus Christ. It made me love a holy life and long to do something for the honor and glory of the name of the Lord Jesus. Yea, I thought that if I had now a thousand gallons of blood in my body, I could spill it all for the sake of the Lord Jesus."

Chapter Fourteen

STUBBORN IGNORANCE

I then saw in my dream that Hopeful looked back and noticed Ignorance, whom they had left behind, still following them. "Look how far the youngster follows behind us," he said to Christian.

"Yes, I see him," said Christian, "but he does not care for our company."

Hopeful added, "Yet I don't think it would have hurt him if he had walked along with us all this time."

Christian said, "That is true. Our companionship might have done him well, but I am sure he thinks otherwise."

"I think you are right," Hopeful stated. "However, let's wait for him."

So they did.

Then Christian said to Ignorance, "Hurry up, man. Why do you lag behind?"

Ignorance answered, "I take pleasure in walking alone and enjoy it more than traveling in the company of others, unless I really like the particular members of such company."

Then Christian said to Hopeful, softly, "Didn't I tell you he cared not for our company?" Then, turning to Ignorance, Christian said to him, "Come along with us, and let us spend our time talking as we walk through this solitary place." Then he inquired of Ignorance, saying, "How are you doing? How stands it between God and your soul now?"

Ignorance replied, "I hope well, for I am always full of good thoughts and intentions that come into my mind that comfort me as I walk."[a]

"What good thoughts and intentions?" Christian inquired. "Please, tell us."

"Why, I think of God and Heaven."

"So do the devils and damned souls," Christian pointed out.

Ignorance added, "But I think of them and also desire them."

Christian asserted, "So do many who are never going to make it to Heaven. 'The soul of the sluggard desires, and hath nothing.'"[b]

"But I think of them and leave all that I possess and enjoy that I might gain them," Ignorance claimed.

"I doubt that," Christian exclaimed, "since leaving all is a hard matter. It is a much harder matter than many are aware of. But what is it that persuades you that you have left all for God and Heaven?"

"My heart tells me so."

Christian challenged, "The wise man says, 'He that trusts his own heart is a fool.'"[c]

"This is spoken of an evil heart, but mine is a good one," Ignorance insisted.

Christian quickly asked, "But how can you prove that?"

Ignorance asserted, "It comforts me with hopes of Heaven."

"That may be your heart deceiving you," Christian warned. "A man's heart may comfort him with hopes of things that, in all truth, he has no reason to hope for."

Ignorance insisted, "But my heart and life agree together, and therefore my hope is well-grounded."

[a]Proverbs 28:26.
[b]Proverbs 13:4.
[c]Proverbs 28:26.

"Who told you that your heart and life agree together?"

"My heart tells me so," Ignorance claimed strongly.

Christian suggested, "Then ask your heart if I am a thief. Your heart may tell you that I am, but that does not make it so. Unless the Word of God bears witness in this matter, no other testimony is of value."

"But is it not a good heart that has good thoughts?" Ignorance questioned. "And isn't a good life one that is lived according to God's commandments?"

"Yes, a good heart has good thoughts, and a good life is one lived according to God's commandments," Christian agreed, adding, "But it is one thing, indeed, to have these and another thing only to think you do."

Ignorance said, "Please tell me what you consider to be good thoughts and a life lived according to God's commandments."

Christian replied, "There are good thoughts pertaining to different things, some with respect to ourselves, God, Christ, and other things."

"What do you think are good thoughts in relation to ourselves?" Ignorance inquired.

Christian answered, "Such as agree with the Word of God."

"What kind of thoughts about ourselves agree with the Word of God?" Ignorance asked further.

Christian explained, "We think rightly of ourselves when we pass the same judgment upon ourselves that the Word passes. To explain myself more fully, the Word of God says of persons in a natural condition, 'There is none righteous, there is none that doeth good.'[d] It also says that 'every imagination of the heart of man is only evil, and that continually.'[e] And again, 'The imagination of man's heart is evil from his youth.'[f] Now then, when we think these thoughts of ourselves, our thoughts are good ones because they agree with the Word of God."

---

[d]Romans 3:10, 12.
[e]Genesis 6:5.
[f]Genesis 8:21.

Ignorance insisted, "I will never believe that my heart is that bad."

"Therefore you have never had one good thought concerning yourself in your entire life," Christian exclaimed. "But let me go on. As the Word passes judgment upon our heart, so it passes judgment upon our ways. When the thoughts concerning our hearts and ways agree with the judgment that the Word gives of both, then are both thoughts good, because they agree with the Word."

"Tell me what you mean," Ignorance urged.

Christian went on, "Why, the Word of God says that man's ways are crooked ways; not good, but perverse.[g] It says that man is naturally opposed to the good way and cannot know it.[h] Now, when a man knows in his head and humbly believes with all his heart that the Word is right and that his ways are not good, then he has good thoughts regarding his own ways because his thoughts now agree with the judgment of the Word of God."

"What are good thoughts concerning God?"

Christian went on, "Just as our thoughts of ourselves are good when they agree with the Word of God, so are they good thoughts concerning God when they agree with what the Word says of Him. We must agree with the Word when it teaches us about the attributes of God, which are too large a subject to talk about right now. In reference to ourselves, we have right thoughts about God when we understand that He knows us better than we know ourselves and can see the sin in us when we can see none. Our thoughts concerning God are good when we understand that He knows our inmost thoughts and that our heart, with all its depths, is always clearly seen by Him. Our thoughts about God are good when we think that all our righteousness stinks in His nostrils and that therefore He cannot stand to see us come before Him in our own confidence, even with all our best performances."

Ignorance asked, "Do you think that I am such a fool as to think

[g]Psalm 125; Proverbs 2:15.
[h]Romans 3.

God can see no further than I? Or that I would come to God in the confidence of my best performances?"

"So what do you think on this matter?" Christian asked back.

Ignorance replied, "To be short, I think I must believe in Christ for justification."

"How is it that you think you must believe in Christ when you do not see your need for Him?" Christian questioned. "You neither see your original nor actual infirmities. You have an opinion of yourself and of your deeds that puts you in a category of man who sees no necessity for Christ's personal righteousness to justify you before God. How can you say that you believe in Christ?"

Ignorance insisted, "In spite of what you say, I believe."

"But what do you believe?" Christian inquired.

Ignorance asserted, "I believe that Christ died for sinners and that I shall be justified before God from the curse through His gracious acceptance of my obedience to His law. I believe that Christ makes my religious duties acceptable to His Father, by virtue of His merits, and so shall I be justified."

"Let me discuss your confession of faith," Christian offered. "First, you believe with a fantasy faith, for this faith is nowhere described in the Word. You also believe with a false faith that takes justification away from the personal righteousness of Christ and credits it to you. The faith you describe makes Christ a justifier of your actions, not of your person. Thus, according to this faith, you are justified by your actions, which is false. Therefore, this faith is deceitful and will leave you under God's wrath in the Day of Judgment.

"True justifying faith makes the soul aware of its lost condition under the Law. The soul that comes to the righteousness of Christ for refuge understands that it is Christ's righteousness alone that is acceptable to God. It is not a mixture of both Christ's obedience and our attempts at obedience that justify us to God. Your obedience is worthless and full of sin, and it is only the obedience of Jesus Christ that God accepts as payment for your sin. True faith causes the soul to flee underneath the righteousness of Christ for relief from the condemnation that we deserve, and it is Christ's righteousness alone that will be presented as spotless before God and accepted by Him as payment for our debt of sin."

"What!" Ignorance exclaimed. "Would you have us trust in what Christ alone has accomplished without adding our own accomplishments? Believing in Christ and His righteousness would give us complete abandon to live as we choose the moment we believed it. This way of thinking would loosen the reins of our lust and permit us to disobey God's commands to our heart's content."

"Ignorance is your name, and as your name is, so are you," Christian exclaimed. "Your answer demonstrates what I say. You are ignorant of what justifying righteousness is, and you are ignorant of how to secure your soul through faith from the heavy wrath of God. Yes, and you are also ignorant of the true effects of saving faith in the righteousness of Christ, the effects of which are to bend and win over the heart to God in Christ. The heart won over to Him will love His name, His Word, His ways, and His people. Saving faith will not, as you ignorantly imagine, give license to do evil but will instead give the earnest desire and power to do good."

Hopeful added, "Ask him if he ever had Christ revealed to him from Heaven."

"What! You are a man who believes in revelations?" Ignorance protested. "I believe that what both of you, and all the rest of your kind, say about that matter is the fruit of a distracted brain."

Hopeful went on, "Why, man? Christ is so hidden in God from the natural apprehensions of the flesh that He cannot by any man be rightly and savingly known unless God the Father reveals Him to them."

"That is your faith, but not mine," Ignorance asserted. "I believe that my faith is as good as yours, although it does not fill my head with so many whimsical ideas as your faith does."

Christian spoke up. "Give me a moment to put in a word. You ought not to speak so lightly of this matter. For this I will boldly affirm, even as my good companion has done, that no man can know Jesus Christ except by the revelation of the Father.[i] Even faith also, by which the soul lays hold upon Christ, if it is right and good faith, must be wrought by the exceeding greatness of His mighty power. I perceive, poor Ignorance, that you are also ignorant of how true saving faith works its effects in the life of a true believer.[j] Wake up, see your own wretchedness, and fly to the Lord Jesus. He is the righteousness of God, for He Himself is God. Only by believing in His righteousness will you be delivered from condemnation."

"You are going too fast," Ignorance complained. "I cannot keep pace with you. You go on ahead. I must stay behind for a while."

Then they said, "Well, Ignorance, will you remain foolish? Will you ignore the good counsel given to you over and over again? And if you still refuse it, you shall know before very long the evil of your doing so. Remember, good counsel that is taken can save you, so listen to us. But if you disregard it, you will be the loser, Ignorance. We promise you that."

Then Christian addressed Hopeful. "Come, my good Hopeful. I perceive that you and I must walk by ourselves again."

So I saw in my dream that they went on ahead, and Ignorance came hobbling after them. Then Christian said to his companion, "I pity this poor man; it will not go well for him in the end."

"What a shame!" Hopeful lamented. "There is an abundance of people in our town in his same condition, entire families and even entire streets, and some are pilgrims. And if there are so many in our town, just think how many there must be in the place where Ignorance was born!"

Christian added, "Indeed, the Word says, 'He has blinded their eyes, lest they should see.'[k] But now that we are by ourselves, tell me what you think of such men. Do you think that they have ever felt the weight of conviction of their sin and the consequent fear that they might be in a dangerous state?"

---

[i] Matthew 11:27.
[j] 1 Corinthians 12:3; Ephesians 1:18–19.
[k] John 12:40.

"I would prefer you answer the question yourself, since you're my elder and more experienced," Hopeful stated.

Christian continued, "I believe that they may sometimes come under the conviction of sin; but being naturally ignorant, they do not understand that such conviction is for their good. Therefore they desperately seek to stifle them and presumptuously continue to flatter themselves that their way of thinking in their own hearts is correct."

"I believe that you are right and that fear would do these men much good in truly preparing them to go on this pilgrimage," Hopeful agreed.

Christian said, "Without a doubt the right fear can be a good thing, for as the Word says, 'The fear of the Lord is the beginning of wisdom.'"[1]

"How would you describe right fear?" Hopeful inquired.

Christian explained, "True or right fear can be known by three things. First, by what causes it: the right kind of fear is caused by saving conviction of sin. Secondly, a good fear drives the soul to quickly lay hold of Christ for salvation. And thirdly, this fear begins and sustains in the soul a great reverence for God, His Word, and His ways. It keeps the soul tender, making it afraid to turn right or left from His Word and ways. It makes the soul sensitive to anything that might dishonor God, grieve the Spirit, or cause the enemy to speak against God."

Hopeful stated, "Well said. I believe you have told the truth. Are we almost past the Enchanted Ground?"

"Why, are you tired of this discourse?"

"No," Hopeful said, "truly I just wanted to know where we are."

"We have a little over two miles farther to go. But let's get back to our conversation." Christian continued, "Now the ignorant do not understand that the conviction of sin that makes them fearful is for their own good, and so they try to stifle all such fears."

"How do they try to stifle them?" Hopeful asked.

---

[1]Proverbs 1:7; 9:10; Psalm 111:10; Job. 28:28.

Christian answered, "First of all, they think that those fears are caused by the Devil (even though they are caused by God); and so they resist them as they would anything else they consider destructive. Secondly, they also think that these fears would spoil their faith, when the truth is that these poor men have no real faith to spoil. So they harden their hearts against all such fears. Thirdly, they presume they ought not to fear; and therefore despite their fear they behave in willful self-confidence. Last of all, they see that those fears tend to take away their own personal merit that they imagine they have as a result of their pitiful old self-holiness, and therefore they resist them with all their might."

Hopeful stated, "I know something of this myself, for before I knew better, it was so with me."

"Well, we will leave the topic of our neighbor Ignorance for the time being and discuss another profitable question," Christian suggested.

"Gladly," Hopeful agreed, "but you begin."

"Did you know a man named Temporary who lived in your parts about ten years ago?" Christian asked. "He was a devoutly religious man back then."

Hopeful replied, "Oh, yes, I did know him. He lived in the town of Graceless about two miles away from the town of Honesty. He lived next to Mr. Turnback."

"Right," Christian said. "Those two lived under the same roof. Well, that man was at one time much awakened to the seriousness of his own sin and of the wages that were due them."

"I think you are right," Hopeful confirmed, "for my house was only three miles from him, and he would often come to visit me when in distress and full of tears. Truly I pitied the man and was not altogether without hope for him. But then again, not every one who cries, 'Lord, Lord' . . ."

Christian went on, "He told me once that he was resolved to go on pilgrimage as we are now. But all of a sudden he grew acquainted with Mr. Save-Self, and then he became a stranger to me."

"Since we are talking about him, let's discuss the reasons why he and others like him suddenly backslide," Hopeful suggested.

"That would be a profitable discussion. You begin."

"Well then, there are in my judgment four reasons for it," Hopeful asserted. "The first reason would be that though the consciences of such men are awakened, their minds are not changed. Thus when the power of guilt fades away and those things that provoked them to be religious stop, they naturally turn to their own course again. It is like the sick dog who vomits what he has eaten and casts it all out, not because he has a mind to do so, but only because his stomach is upset. When the upset stomach goes away, the dog returns to his vomit and licks it up, and so it is true, as is written, 'The dog is turned to his own vomit again.'[m] I conclude that if they long for Heaven only by virtue of their fear of the torments of Hell, then as their sense of Hell and the fears of damnation chill and cool, so do their desires for Heaven and salvation cool also. So then it comes to pass that when their guilt and fear are gone, their desires for Heaven and happiness die, and they return to their former ways again.

"A second reason for backsliding is that they have slavish fears that control them. I am talking about the fears that they have of men, for 'the fear of man brings a snare.'[n] So then, though they seem to long earnestly for Heaven while the flames of Hell are about their ears, yet when that terror is over, they have second thoughts. They begin to think that it is good to be 'wise' in the worldly sense and not run the hazard of losing it all, or at the very least of bringing themselves into avoidable and unnecessary troubles. Because of their fear of what man might do to an honest pilgrim, they fall in with the world again.

"The next reason for backsliding is the shame that attends true religion, which makes it a stumbling block to them. They are proud and haughty and consider true religion to be low and contemptible.

[m]2 Peter 2:22.
[n]Proverbs 29:25.

When they have lost their sense of Hell and wrath to come, they return to their former course.

"Lastly, the guilt and terror that come to mind as they consider their own miserable condition is something that grieves them. But it does not cause them to fly to Christ for safety; no, instead it causes them to try to avoid all such terrible thoughts. When their awakening to the terrors and wrath of God fade away, then they choose ways that will harden them to any such awakening in the future."

Christian said, "You have summed it up well. At the bottom of it all is the simple truth that these men never change their will or their mind. That is, they never truly repent. They are like the criminal who stands before the judge quaking and trembling. He seems to genuinely repent, but at the bottom of it all is a fear of prison, not any real remorse for his crimes. If he is set free, he will return to his criminal activity. If his mind had truly been changed, he would stop being a criminal."

"Now that I have shown you the reasons for their backsliding, you show me the manner in which they do it," Hopeful challenged.

"I will," Christian agreed. "First of all, the backsliders resist all thoughts of God, death, and the judgment to come. Thus, to continue this resistance, they begin by degrees to cast off private duties such as closet prayer, curbing their lusts, watching their souls, grieving over their sin, and the like. They also begin to shun the company of lively and warm Christians.

"After this mostly private resistance, they then grow cold to their public duties such as hearing God's Word preached, reading the Bible, and assembling together with other Christians. They start to abandon the assembly of believers, finding fault with other Christians, often naming them hypocrites, in order to provide an excuse for leaving them.

"Having abandoned the fellowship of the saints, they then begin to draw close to and associate themselves with fleshly, loose, greedy, lewd, and unruly men. This new company tempts them to give way to fleshly and lewd practices, at first in secret. They are glad if they can find any fault or sin in those they once considered honest, using them as an excuse and example to justify their own sins.

"After this season of private sin, they begin to play with certain sins openly. Finally then, being hardened, they show themselves for what they are. Then they are launched again into the gulf of misery, and unless a miracle of grace prevents it, they perish forever in their own deceit."

Chapter Fifteen

HOME IN THE CELESTIAL CITY

ow I saw in my dream that by this time the pilgrims had passed over the Enchanted Ground and entered into the country of Beulah, whose air was very sweet and pleas-ant.[1] Since the way went directly through Beulah, the pilgrims found comfort and relief as they traveled through this country.[a] Here they heard the continual singing of birds, saw flowers appear on the earth, and heard the voice of the turtledove in the land.[b] In this country the sun shone night and day.[2] Beulah was beyond the Valley of the Shadow of Death and also out of the reach of Giant Despair, nor could they even see Doubting Castle from this place.

Here they were within sight of the City to which they were going. They also met some of the inhabitants of the country, for in this land the Shining Ones commonly walked because it was upon the borders of Heaven.[3] In this land also the contract between the bride and the Bridegroom was renewed: "As the bridegroom rejoiceth over the bride, so did their God rejoice over them."[c] Here they had no lack of bread or wine, for in this place they met with an abundance of

---

[a]Isaiah 62:4.
[b]Song 2:10–12.
[c]Isaiah 62:5.

what they had sought during all their pilgrimage.[d] Here they heard voices from outside the City, loud voices proclaiming, "Say ye to the daughter of Zion, 'Behold, thy salvation cometh! Behold, His reward is with Him!'"[e] Here all the inhabitants of the country called them "the holy people, the redeemed of the Lord, those sought out."[f4]

Now as they walked in this land, they rejoiced more than they had in any other part of the journey. And as they came near the Celestial City, they could see that it was built of pearls and precious stones and that the streets were paved with gold. The natural glory of the City and the sunbeams' reflection on it made Christian feel sick with desire. Hopeful also had a few bouts of the same sickness. The sickness was so great that they had to rest from their journey while crying out because of the deep pangs of desire: "If ye find my Beloved, tell Him that I am sick with love."[g]

Finally they got some of their strength back and were able to bear their sickness. As they walked on their way, coming even nearer to the City, they came upon orchards, vineyards, and gardens that were opened to the highway. It was there that they saw a gardener standing in the path. The pilgrims asked him, "Whose lovely vineyards and gardens are these?"

He answered, "They are the King's and are planted here for His own delight, and also for the solace of pilgrims." So the gardener invited them into the vineyards and told them to refresh themselves.[h] He also showed them the King's favorite walkways and the arbors; and here they tarried and slept.

Now I beheld in my dream that during this time Christian and Hopeful talked more in their sleep than they ever did during the entire journey. The reason for this is that the grapes of these vineyards go down so sweetly that they cause the lips of those who sleep to speak.

So I saw that when they awoke, they prepared to go up to the

---

[d]Isaiah 62:8.
[e]Isaiah 62:11.
[f]Isaiah 62:12.
[g]Song 5:8.
[h]Deuteronomy 23:24.

City.[5] But the reflection of the sun upon the City (for "the city was pure gold"[i]) was so extremely glorious that they could not behold it without covering their eyes. They could only see it by looking through an instrument made for just that purpose.[j] So I saw that as they went on, they met two men whose raiment shone like gold and whose faces shone as the light.

These men asked the pilgrims where they came from, and they told them. They also asked them where they had lodged, what difficulties and dangers, what comforts and pleasures they had met on the way. After listening to their answers, the men who met them said, "You have only two more difficulties to overcome, and then you are in the City."

Then Christian and his companion asked the men to go along with them, so they told them they would. "But," they said, "you must enter the City by your own faith." So I saw in my dream that they went on together until they came within sight of the gate.

Now between them and the gate was a river, but there was no bridge to go over, and the river was very deep. At the sight of this river, the pilgrims were stunned. Then the men who went with them said, "You must go through the river or you cannot enter into the City at the gate."

The pilgrims then began to inquire if there were no other way to the gate, to which they answered, "Yes, but there have only been two, Enoch and Elijah, permitted to tread that path since the foundation of the world. And no one else will be permitted to go that way until the last trumpet shall sound."[k6]

Then the pilgrims, especially Christian, began to despair in their minds. They looked this way and that, but no way could be found to escape the river.

Then they asked the men if the waters were deep everywhere all the time. They told them that sometimes the water was shallow, but that they could not guide them in that matter since the

---

[i]Revelation 21:18.
[j]2 Corinthians 3:18.
[k]1 Corinthians 15:51–52.

waters were deep or shallow depending upon their faith in the King of the place.

Then they waded into the water, and upon entering, Christian began to sink. He cried out to his good friend Hopeful, saying, "I am sinking in deep waters; the billows are going over my head, all his waves go over me! Selah."[17]

Then Hopeful said, "Be of good cheer, my brother. I feel the bottom, and it is good."

Then Christian cried out, "Ah, my friend! 'The sorrows of death have compassed me about.'[m] I shall not see the land that flows with milk and honey."

With that a great darkness and horror fell upon Christian, so that he could not see ahead.

It was then that Christian lost his senses, and his memory failed him, and he could not talk in an orderly fashion of any of those sweet refreshments that he had met with in the way of his pilgrimage.

All the words that he spoke were filled with horror, and he feared that he should die in that river and never obtain entrance at the gate. He was greatly troubled by thoughts of his past sins, committed before and during his pilgrimage. It was also observed that he was troubled with apparitions of hobgoblins and evil spirits, which he continually spoke about.

It was everything that Hopeful could do to keep his brother's head above water. Sometimes Christian, despite all Hopeful's help, would slip down into the waters and rise up again half-dead.

Hopeful continually tried to comfort him, saying, "Brother, I see the gate, and men standing by to receive us."

But Christian would answer, "It is you, it is you they wait for. You have been Hopeful ever since I knew you."

"And so have you," Hopeful said to Christian.

---

[l] Psalm 69:2.
[m] Psalm 18:5.

Christian and Hopeful cross over the River of Death.

Christian answered, "If things were right with me, He would now come to help me, but because of my sin He has brought me to this snare, and He will leave me here."

Then said Hopeful, "My brother, you have forgotten the text where it is said of the wicked, 'There are no bands in their death; but their strength is firm. They are not in trouble as other men, neither are they plagued like other men.'[n] These troubles and distresses that you are going through in these waters are not a sign that God has forsaken you but are sent to try you, to see if you will call to mind all the goodness that you have received from Him. You are being tested to see if you will rely on Him in your distress."

Then I saw in my dream that Christian was in a bewildered stupor for a while. Hopeful spoke to Christian, encouraging him to "Be of good cheer," reminding him that Jesus Christ would make him whole.

With that Christian shouted out with a loud voice, "Oh, I see Him again, and He tells me, 'When you pass through the waters, I will be with you; and through the rivers, they will not overflow you.'"[o]

Then they both took courage and crossed the river, and the enemy was as still as a stone. Christian soon found solid ground to stand on, and the rest of the river was shallow. So Christian and Hopeful crossed over the river and arrived on the other side. As soon as they came out of the river, they saw the two shining men again waiting for them. The men saluted the two pilgrims saying, "We are ministering spirits, sent here to minister to those who shall be heirs of salvation."[p] Then they all went along together toward the gate.

Now though the City stood upon a mighty hill with its foundations higher than the clouds, the pilgrims went up with ease, agility, and speed because the ministering spirits supported their arms as they led them. Also, they had left their mortal garments behind

---

[n]Psalm 73:4–5.
[o]Isaiah 43:2.
[p]Hebrews 1:14.

them in the river, for though they had gone in with them, they had come out without them.

They went up through the regions of the air, sweetly talking as they went, being comforted because they had safely crossed over the river and had such glorious companions to assist them.

They spoke about the glory of the place with the Shining Ones, who replied that the beauty and glory of it was inexpressible.[9] Then they said that it was "'Mount Zion, the heavenly Jerusalem, the innumerable company of angels, and the spirits of just men made perfect.'[q] "You are going now," they said, "to the Paradise of God, wherein you shall see the tree of life and eat of its never-fading fruits. When you come there, you shall have white robes given to you, and you shall walk and talk every day with the King, even all the days of eternity.[r] There you shall not see again such things as you saw when you were in the lower region upon the earth. You will not see sorrow, sickness, affliction, and death, 'for the former things are passed away.'[s] You are now going to Abraham, Isaac, and Jacob and to the prophets, men whom God has taken away from the evil to come and who are now resting upon their beds, each one walking in his righteousness."[t]

Christian and Hopeful asked, "What must we do in the holy place?"

The Shining Ones answered, "You must receive the comforts of all your toil and have joy for all your sorrow; you must reap what you have sown, even the fruit of all your prayers, tears, and sufferings in your journey for the King. In that place you must wear crowns of gold and enjoy the perpetual sight and vision of the Holy One, for 'there you shall see Him as He is.'[u] There also you shall serve Him continually with praise, shouting, and thanksgiving, Him whom you desired to serve in the world, though with much difficulty, because of the infirmity of your flesh. There your eyes shall

---

[q]Hebrews 12:22–24.
[r]Revelation 2:7; 3:4; 22:5.
[s]Revelation 21:4.
[t]Isaiah 57:1–2; 65:17.
[u]1 John 3:2.

be delighted with seeing, and your ears with hearing the pleasant voice of the Mighty One. There you shall enjoy your friends again, those who have gone before you, and there you shall with joy receive all those who follow you to this holy place.

"You shall also be clothed with glory and majesty and ride with the King of glory in His royal carriage. When He shall come with the sound of the trumpet in the clouds, as upon the wings of the wind, you shall also come with Him. And when He shall sit upon the throne of judgment, you shall sit by Him. Yea, and when He passes sentence upon all the workers of iniquity, whether angels or men, you also shall have a voice in that judgment, because they were His and your enemies.[v] Also when He shall again return to the City with the sound of the trumpet, you shall go too and be ever with Him."

Now while they were thus drawing toward the gate, a company of the heavenly host came out to meet them, to which the Shining Ones who attended Christian and Hopeful said, "These are the men who have loved our Lord when they were in the world and who have left all for His holy name. He has sent us to fetch them, and we have brought them to the very place they have desired to be, that they may go in and look their Redeemer in the face with joy."

Then the heavenly host gave a great shout, saying, "Blessed are they who are called unto the marriage supper of the Lamb."[w] There came out also at this time to meet them several of the King's trumpeters, clothed in white and shining raiment. They made loud, melodious noises that made the heavens echo with their sound. With shouting and the sounds of trumpets, these trumpeters saluted Christian and his companion with ten thousand welcomes.

After this they surrounded them on every side. Some went before, some behind, some on the right hand, some on the left (so as to guard them through the upper regions), continually making majestic sounds as they went, with melodious noise, in notes on

---

[v]1 Thessalonians 4:13–17; Jude 14; Daniel 7:9–10; 1 Corinthians 6:2–3.
[w]Revelation 19:9.

high. To anyone looking, it would have appeared that Heaven itself had come down to meet them.

And so they walked on together, and as they walked, the trumpeters mixed their joyful music with looks and gestures that signified to Christian and Hopeful how welcome they were in their company. They never stopped telling them how glad they were to meet them.

As the two pilgrims approached Heaven, it seemed to them that they were being swallowed up with the sight of angels and the sound of their melodious music. And it was then that the City itself came into their view, and they thought they heard all the bells in the City ringing to welcome them. But above all, they had warm and joyful thoughts about living there with such company, and that forever and ever. O by what tongue or pen can their glorious joy be expressed! And so they came up to the gate.

Now, when they had come up to the gate, they saw written over it in letters of gold, "Blessed are they who do His commandments, that they may have the right to the tree of life and may enter in through the gates into the City."[x]

Then I saw in my dream that the shining men told them to call at the gate. When they did, Enoch, Moses, and Elijah looked down from over the gate. It was then that someone said to those great men of God, "These pilgrims have come from the City of Destruction for the love that they have for the King of this place." Then Christian and Hopeful gave them their certificates that they had received in the beginning.

The certificates were carried in to the King, who, when He had read them, said, "Where are these men?"

"They are standing outside the gate," came the answer.

The King then commanded them to open the gate, "that the righteous nation," said He, "which keepeth the truth may enter in."[y]

Now I saw in my dream that Christian and Hopeful went in

---

[x]Revelation 22:14.
[y]Isaiah 26:2.

through the gate, and as they entered, they were transfigured and clothed with raiment that shone like gold. There they were met by others with harps and crowns, who gave them harps with which to praise and crowns in token of the King's honor.

Then I heard in my dream all the bells in the City ringing out for joy. Then Christian and Hopeful were told, "Enter ye into the joy of your Lord."

I also heard Christian and Hopeful sing with a loud voice, "Blessing and honor and glory and power be unto Him that sitteth upon the throne, and unto the Lamb, forever and ever."[z]

Now just as the gates were opened to let them in, I looked in myself, and I saw the City shining like the sun. The streets were paved with gold, and on them walked many men with crowns on their heads, palms in their hands, and golden harps to sing praises. There were also among them winged angels, and they shouted to one another continually, proclaiming, "Holy, holy, holy, is the Lord."[aa] And after that, they shut up the gates. Having seen what was inside the gates, I wished that I could join them.

Now while I was looking at all these things, I turned my head to look back and saw Ignorance approaching the river. He crossed without any of the difficulty that Christian and Hopeful had since there was a ferryman named Vain-Hope ready to take him across in his boat.

Once Ignorance arrived on the other side of the river, he ascended the hill just like Christian and Hopeful, except that no one had come to meet him or give him any encouragement as he made his way to the City. When he had come up to the gate, he looked up and read what was written above it. He then began to knock, supposing that he would quickly be invited in.

But instead of the gates opening, he was asked by the men who looked over the top of the gate, "Where did you come from? What do you want?"

[z]Revelation 5:13.
[aa]Revelation 4:8.

Ignorance is deposited in Hell.

Ignorance answered, "I have eaten and have drunk in the presence of the King, and He has taught in our streets." Then they asked him for his certificate, so that they might go in and show it to the King. Ignorance fumbled in his pockets but found nothing. Then they asked, "Don't you have a certificate?" Ignorance made no reply, not a word.

So they told the King, but He would not come down to see him. He commanded the two Shining Ones who had conducted Christian and Hopeful to the City to go out and take Ignorance away, binding him hand and foot. Then they took him up and carried him through the air to the door that I saw in the side of the hill, and in there they put him.

Then I saw that there was a way to Hell from the gates of Heaven as well as from the City of Destruction![10]

So I awoke, and behold, it was a dream.

The Conclusion

Now, Reader,
I have told my dream to thee;
See if you can interpret it to me,
Or to yourself, or to your neighbor; but take heed
Of misinterpreting; for that, instead
Of doing good, will but thyself abuse:
By misinterpreting, evil ensues.

Take heed also, that thou be not extreme,
In playing with the outside of my dream:
Nor let my figure or similitude
Put thee into laughter or a feud.
Leave this for boys and fools; but as for thee,
Do thou the substance of my matter see.

Pull aside the curtains, look within my veil,
Turn over my metaphors, and do not fail;
There, if thou seekest them, such things thou wilt find,
As will be helpful to an honest mind.

What of my dross thou findest there? Be bold
To throw away, but yet preserve the gold;
What if my gold be wrapped up in ore?
None throws away the apple for the core.
But if thou cast all away as vain,
I know not but it will make me dream again.

EDITOR'S NOTES

Chapter One: Pilgrim's Great Distress

1. With all its temporary delights and momentary distractions, to Bunyan the world was a *wilderness*. This is an allusion to the dismal wanderings of Israel in the Sinai desert, where the soul became parched in the withering heat of unbelief. The *cave* was Bedford County Jail, where Bunyan spent twelve long years of his life because of his ardent stand against the stifling authoritarianism of the church-state, which returned in 1660 under the rule of Charles the Second.

2. His clothing of *rags* illustrates that his own righteousness was no better than filthy rags. *His face turned away from his own house* teaches us that the man is looking for help, but this help will not come from his family or from anyone in the city from which he seeks to escape.

3. The *book* the man is reading is the Word of God, the Bible. It has become both the focus of and the reason for his current state of perplexity and distress. The *heavy burden* on his back is his awakened knowledge and sense of his own sin. The man discovers the frightful condition of his heart, which provokes genuine and constant fears of damnation. These fears are an ever-present weight upon his entire person.

4. Christian's first reference to *Heaven* is fearsome and foreboding—the place from which fire falls. He is certain this fire will someday consume and destroy his city, his family, and himself. No promise is found in the book he reads, only certain doom—unless, by a way yet hidden to him, he might escape.

5. Christian's family is confused and alarmed by what they consider the eccentric and unwarranted concerns that Christian now has for the condition and final destination of his eternal soul. They think he has caught some "religious disease" and *is losing his mind*.

6. Christian's first mention of *praying* forecasts the genuineness of the work being done in his heart. To be sure, he is praying for relief from his own misery, but only after he prays for his wife and children. Christian is full of pain but also full of pity. "Graceless" has already begun to fade as "Christian" emerges.

7. Christian's first question, *"What shall I do?"* now flowers into the only question that can successfully launch his journey, *"What shall I do to be saved?"* This question is predicated by his impending sense of danger, his humbled posture under the burden of sin, and his deep desire to receive guidance that will result in both deliverance and peace. If he seeks God's face, it is a muted desire, temporarily overshadowed by his preoccupation with the tragic condition that fills his consciousness with fear and dread.

8. Then Christian meets *Evangelist*. Our current notion of an evangelist probably does not match what Bunyan had in mind. The model for this character was probably Pastor John Gifford of Bedford, an earnest and faithful minister of the gospel. Evangelist is a pastor with compassion for lost souls. He is well-instructed in the saving truths that are only found in God's Word. He does not press unbelievers for a quick decision based on an emotional appeal. Evangelist is a serious man, determined to perform the task of directing sinners to the Savior with a solemn clarity informed only by the "best of books," as it is referred to later, the very Bible that Christian holds in his hands.

9. Evangelist unrolls and reads from the *parchment* the only message that will successfully direct Christian to the Celestial City. The parchment represents the Bible, and in particular those truths in it that implore sinners to repent of their sins and *"Flee from the wrath to come."* Evangelist is imploring Christian to escape by the only way prescribed by God and available to poor sinners, Jesus Christ the Savior. It is He alone

who rescues sinners from the wrath of God. Unfortunately, Christian is still blind to this truth.

10. We can imagine Evangelist asking Christian if he understands the good news. Does Christian understand the mystery of the saving work accomplished on the cross of Christ? Does he see, even when squinting, the relief that can be found in Christ alone? The answer is no.

11. When Evangelist asks Christian, *"Do you see the distant narrow gate?"* he is asking Christian if he understands that Jesus Christ is the only way by which people can enter the place where they will find rest for their souls, forgiveness of sins, and the certain hope of eternal life. In short, does he understand the good news revealed in the book he holds?

   Christian again answers, "No." The mercy found only in Christ could not be seen or understood by poor Christian. The door that one must enter in order to find peace with God was outside the realm of his understanding. Christ, the only way to God the Father, is a narrow gate that most men will never find or enter. Without further revelation Christian is left with a desire to flee from certain wrath, yet with no place of safety to which he can retreat.

   Evangelist is not discouraged by Christian's answer and quickly asks Christian, *"Do you see the distant shining light?"* Evangelist is asking if Christian perceives any glimmer of hope as he reads the illuminating Word of God. The answer Christian gives is the first encouraging sign as Christian responds, "I think I do."

12. Christ cannot be found without the Word, and so Evangelist tells Christian to *"Keep that light in your eye, and go up directly toward it, and soon you will see the narrow gate."* In other words, keep reading the Bible until in it the Son of God is revealed to you.

   How could Evangelist be sure that Christian would find Christ as the reward for his faithful and urgent reading of God's Word? The answer is not presumptuous but rather that Evangelist, being a doctor of the soul, recognized in Christian the genuine working of the Holy Spirit, who had already enlightened poor Christian to his miserable and dangerous condition.

   Evangelist did not try to interfere with Christian's struggle or attempt to end his misery. Instead he recognized the good work that had begun in Christian, and with reverence for God's perfect way of dealing with sinners, he simply encouraged Christian to keep reading the very book that had awakened him to his dark and desperate condition.

13. The actions of *Obstinate* and *Pliable* confirm the simple lesson that the world does not easily or readily give up its citizens. Obstinate represents the intolerant class of people who think it foolish and senseless to give up all the comforts of this world for what they are convinced is nothing more than a fanciful delusion and a waste of time. According to Obstinate, our loyalties should be only to this world—its friendships, opportunities, riches, security, and approval. Obstinate believes the Word of God is unreliable and misleading and pleads for Christian to put his trust in the wisdom that comes from this world rather than in the wisdom that comes from Heaven.

   Pliable represents a different class of people. He is a rudderless ship, a man with mush for a backbone and a faltering will. He has no sense of his own moral failings and lacks anything that would act as a compass for his soul. He is windswept and wave-tossed. He is moved by the moment like butter on a hot plate—easily persuaded and just as easily offended.

14. As Pliable and Christian find themselves walking together toward the narrow gate, we see the stark contrast between the two pilgrims. One is burdened; the other is not. One is clutching a book that is a light to his path. The other is guideless. One is on the journey in pursuit of deliverance from besetting sins and rest for his soul. The other is on the journey in order to obtain future delights that temporarily dazzle his mind. One is slow and plodding because of his great weight and a sense of his own unrighteousness; the other is light-footed and impatient to obtain all the benefits of Heaven. One is

in motion because his soul has been stirred up to both fear and hope; the other is dead to any spiritual fears, longings, or aspirations. One is seeking God; the other is seeking self-satisfaction. One is a true pilgrim; the other is false and fading.

15. It is not surprising that a simple test would separate these two pilgrims forever. Pliable is like the seed that falls on rocky ground in which there is no root or hope of persistence. When the sun blazes hot or the cold winds blow, this rootless plant will wither and blow back to the weed patch that first cradled it.

The opportunity to test these two pilgrims comes in the form of a great miry patch of unsolid ground called the *Swamp of Despond*. After a time of wallowing in this bog and becoming completely shamed by the filth and dirt that polluted that place, Pliable comes to the end of his patience. His dignity disturbed and in a bad temper, Pliable rebukes Christian and struggles out of the mire on the side closest to his own house and nearest to the City of Destruction.

The Swamp of Despond is that place set before the narrow gate where true and false pilgrims alike are assaulted by their own internal corruption and pollution. The dirt and scum that has attached itself to our hearts and minds is agitated and revealed by both the workings of a guilty conscience and the devouring avarice of the enemy of our souls.

The purpose of the Swamp of Despond is to discourage the pilgrim from going forward by putting him in a place that is so vile as to persuade the pilgrim that going forward is too humiliating and ultimately futile. The Swamp of Despond is there to cause despair and shake any conviction that our hope lies just ahead.

The great enemy of grace is the strict accounting of our sin and corruption that when added up totals such a staggering debt that no person without faith in the sure promises of God would ever dare calculate that anything good awaits him and would further be convinced that all that does lie ahead is a complete foreclosure of his soul and all its contents.

Pliable, forced to do the sums while ankle-deep in the Swamp of Despond, is immediately offended by the prospect of his own wickedness and guilt. If the journey begins with this bitter and reprehensible sort of self-disclosure, he calculates it will end only in failure and humiliation.

16. Christian sinks deeper and deeper into the Swamp as he struggles with all his might to get to the side of the Swamp farthest away from the City of Destruction and closest to the narrow gate. Seeing himself as God sees him leaves him deeply discouraged. But even in this hopeless and sinking condition, a glimmer of promise encourages him to move in the direction of the God whose verdict upon his life he now accepts.

17. *Help* arrives on the solid ground outside the swamp with a question and a helping hand: *"Why didn't you look for the steps?"* With fear's full fury blurring Christian's vision, he could not see the steps. What are the steps? They are nothing other than the astounding promises of God. Christian's heart is so filled to overflowing with the fog of fear that he cannot discern the mighty promises that God has made to sinners. Help represents those faithful followers of Christ who strategically station themselves to encourage those seeking to enter the narrow gate. He is the experienced Christian who says with certainty and conviction that you can trust your life to the God who has made solid and trustworthy saving promises to sin-sick sinners. God's promises are always to be relied upon and will always provide a solid footing that keeps the bubbling and belching lies of Satan under feet shod with faith!

Chapter Two: The Way of the World or the Narrow Way

1. Delivered from the Swamp of Despond and on his way to the narrow gate, Christian now crosses paths with *Mr. Worldly-Wiseman*. We discover that Mr. Worldly-Wiseman is from the town of *Carnal Policy*, which further helps clarify the person Bunyan had in mind.

2. A current version of Mr. Worldly-Wiseman is any liberal, broad-minded, and compromising person who has no regard for the atoning work of Jesus Christ and would rather believe a "gospel" advancing morality and social reform. Note how he relishes and makes sport of undermining the biblical convictions that Christian has come so recently to rely on.

3. While Obstinate was brash and coarse in his criticism of the beliefs held by Christian, Mr. Worldly-Wiseman is much more civil and polished in his attack. He pretends sympathy when his real motivation is a hatred for all things touching on the saving work of Christ. His advice is aimed at the temporal and sensory felt needs of Christian, who is persuaded that the removal of his burden is the main aim of his pilgrimage. Mr. Worldly-Wiseman's goal is to focus on the newly awakened feelings that trouble Christian. His goal is to persuade Christian that the elimination of his sense of burden is all that stands between him and a happy ending to his misbegotten journey.

4. Christian is advised not to probe too deeply into the Word of God or to pay any heed to men such as Evangelist, since men who do are often unnecessarily awakened and alarmed to perils that Mr. Worldly-Wiseman waves off as the over-imaginings of a weak mind. All his carnal advice reflects a deep hatred for the saving work of Christ. If he is successful, Christian will loathe the cross of Christ and will be permanently inoculated from the luminous truth about both his condition and eternity.

5. The charm and subtle, seductive manners of Mr. Worldly-Wiseman quickly disarm Christian who is too inexperienced and inattentive to realize that he is being prepared to abandon God altogether and replace Him with idols of morality and legality.

6. When the desire to get rid of the sensory symptoms of sin so that one can live a life of peace and safety is the only goal, and that goal is achieved by a work other than the work of Christ, the end may be peace in this life but God's certain wrath in the world to come. Mr. Worldly-Wiseman is a friend to sinners who want to lose their sense of sin, but the sworn enemy to all who desire lasting peace and eternal life.

7. The hill represents Mt. Sinai where all the demands of the Law, including perfect obedience to them, is required in order to escape the impeccable wrath of God. Christian has already been awakened to the true sense of his own condition. As a result of the inner work of God's convicting Spirit, there is no possible way that Christian can ever again fall into a self-delusion regarding his own righteousness or ability to merit the favor of God.

8. Mr. Worldly-Wiseman is not an ancient relic of the past. He is everywhere today, disguising his heresy and error by proclaiming the gospel of contentment and peace achieved by self-satisfaction and works. If he mentions Christ, it is not as the Savior who took our place, but as a good example of an exemplary life. Do we need a good example to rescue us, or do we need a Savior? If Christian had considered this question carefully earlier, he might have avoided the nearly deadly detour that Mr. Worldly-Wiseman so confidently and cunningly recommended.

9. Who is *Good-Will*? He is a picture of Jesus Himself—God's own goodwill toward sinners—Jesus who welcomes burdened sinners with grace and mercy. It is Jesus who rescues sinners. Jesus pulls them to Himself to protect them from the *arrows* of Satan.

10. Charles Spurgeon considers the fiery arrows to include the satanic suggestion that the magnitude and nature of our sins are so egregious as to disqualify us in particular from the mercy offered in general, that the Holy Spirit has been offended too many times by our past refusals, and that too many invitations to experience grace have been mocked for us to now expect salvation.

    Satan suggests that perhaps we are not one of God's elect, a weed seed that has taken root and infected many with its prickly thorns of doubt. Or perhaps we have committed the unpardonable sin. Maybe we are too insignificant to warrant the merciful attentions of the Savior. Satan has an arsenal of lies each fashioned like arrows to delay, pierce, pain, and discourage the sinner from ever seeking the Savior. The Lord Jesus invites *all* who are weary and heavy-laden to come to Him and find rest for the soul.

11. There is no question that Bunyan means for us to understand that Christian is converted upon entering the narrow gate, which is a picture of Christ. So why does Christian not lose his burden? This answer is important. Remember that the burden is not sin but Christian's sense of it.

    Christian has upon entering into Christ, receiving Him with faith and trust, been legally delivered from the consequences of sin. That being an established fact does not mean that he has been delivered from his own sense of sin, and as a matter of fact Christian remains sensible to it all the same. He has a saving understanding of the work Christ did on the cross, but not a sensible experience of that work done on his behalf. In time Christian will lose his burden, but only after he, in a fuller revelation of the meaning of the cross, comes to more completely understand and apprehend the grace of God.

12. Bunyan tells the truth here. Many come to Christ with little faith and are received by Christ and are forgiven for all their sins; yet they remain in a perplexed state of guilt and shame until the day they fully grasp the grace of God. Others know and experience salvation by forgiveness and all its sensible implications without any delay.

    God's grace is the most incredible and insurmountable truth ever to be revealed to the human heart, which is why God has given us His Holy Spirit to superintend the process of more fully revealing the majesty of the work done on our behalf by our Savior. He teaches us to first cling to, and then enables us to adore with the faith He so graciously supplies, the mercy of God. This mercy has its cause and effect in the work of Jesus on the cross.

13. We can thank Bunyan for telling the truth here, as many have been encouraged to know that the God who instantly justifies us is also in the process of perfecting our faith. He has begun a work, and He will complete that work in His perfect time.

14. Christian is now directed by Good-Will to the *house of the Interpreter*. By this Bunyan shows the regenerative work of the Holy Spirit who shines light on things that were previously darkened. Christian will soon receive understanding about the gospel that will fill his soul with wonder, warnings, amazement, and praise.

15. After interviewing Christian and investigating the genuineness of his conversion, the Interpreter gives Christian insight into seven profitable images of truth.

    1. A *picture* of a solemn and serious person hanging on the wall. This is the picture of a true gospel pastor. The elements of the picture are there for us to contemplate the marks of a true and faithful pastor.

    2. A *parlor* full of dust—a lesson about the difference between the Law and the gospel. One stirs up the noxious reality of sin, while the other cleanses us from its power and presence in our life.

    3. Two children named *Passion* and *Patience*. This is instruction to point out the eternal virtue of patience and the calamitous end of passion.

    4. A *fireplace*. This teaches us that the grace of God, though often hidden and out of sight, will overcome the assaults of Satan and the world.

    5. *Entering into the palace*. This is a picture of a victorious pilgrim who is preserved and given victory and entry into God's Kingdom by the grace of God.

    6. The *iron cage* is a warning to all who would make light of God's promises. This man has made an idol of remorse, despair, and bitterness, never truly crying out to the Lord for mercy because he has decided that God will not hear him or respond to him favorably. He worships his sorrow and has elevated his unbelief above the promises of God. He cannot truly repent because God withholds His mercy from those who make an idol out of unbelief.

    7. A *trembling* man. The crisp and indisputable lesson here is: be prepared for the final judgment!

    All these illuminations encourage Christian to both hope and fear. As a pilgrim on the King's Highway to the Celestial City, Christian must be ready and alert.

Chapter Three: A Burden Lifted and a Journey Begun

1. The *highway* is walled on both sides to indicate that for Christian, the way forward is secure and certain. After experiencing all the uncertainties and spiritual upheaval surrounding his conversion, the path ahead is well-defined and clear. Christian is about to experience deliverance and relief from the burden that has so grieved his soul. Christian fixes his eyes on the *cross* of Christ, and his burden falls off his back.

2. Christian now perceives the atonement and knows without any doubt that Christ's redemptive work on the cross is completely sufficient to satisfy the righteous wrath of God. Christian has come to understand the heart of the gospel. The Savior's blood has accomplished for him what nothing else could—deliverance from the burden and penalty of sin.

3. For the sake of Christ, God has made peace with the pilgrim, Christian. Christian is justified and is forgiven of all his sins. Christian is stripped of his rags and is given a robe of righteousness, which represents the imputed righteousness of Jesus Christ. Christian is given a *mark* on his forehead that sets him apart from the world and marks him as a true child of God who will be preserved from divine judgment. Christian is given a *scroll* with a seal on it, which represents his temporal assurance of his new life and acceptance into the Celestial City.

4. Loosed of his burden, Christian makes his way to the bottom of the hill where he finds three men fast asleep. *Foolish* represents spiritual dullness and ignorance. *Sloth* represents spiritual laziness. *Presumption* represents spiritual pride and arrogance. The consequences of all three conditions are self-inflicted incarceration and lack of progress on the King's Highway.

5. Christian's attempt to help remedy the perilous condition of these three sleeping pilgrims is met with indifference, indolence, and intolerance. Christian, troubled by the lack of spiritual concern in the "religious" world, does his best to bring about a change, but all his efforts are scorned and rebuffed. Lesson one for the new Christian—many a careless and indifferent traveler will not survive the pilgrimage.

6. Christian meets two more ill-fated pilgrims as he continues his expedition down the King's Highway. His ability to discern a false pilgrim has been advanced since his experience with Simple, Sloth, and Presumption.

    Christian immediately focuses on three things that seem out of place. First, the tumbling over the wall called Salvation without coming through Christ, the narrow gate, or experiencing any illumination by the Holy Spirit immediately warns Christian that these are trespassers. Second, their testimony of having come from the land of *Vain-Glory* warns Christian that they are neither humble nor burdened by sin. Third, their wish to arrive at Mt. Zion to *receive* praise rather than to *give* praise to the only one worthy of praise alarms Christian. Christian quickly discerns that the motives of *Formalist* and *Hypocrisy* are unworthy and contemptuous.

    Formalist represents the man who performs many outward religious duties but lacks any inward conviction. The condition of his heart is of little concern to Formalist; everything is external pomp and circumstance.

    Hypocrisy represents the man who has persuaded others and perhaps even himself that he is righteous. He revels in deception and making false appearances. His is a fancy religion when he is in church or among other Christians but ungodly and devilish when out of their sight—all light without any heat.

    Christian notices the differences between the nature of his pilgrimage, which is accredited by the Word of God, and theirs, which is not. He is different than Formalist and Hypocrisy in how he thinks, what he loves, and what he purposes in his heart to do.

    And finally Christian is uniquely different because he does not boast in his own righteousness but only in the righteousness of Christ as represented by the coat on his back. He is marked out as a child of God by the mark on his forehead and is assured of his good standing by the scroll he was given by the three Shining Ones.

7. Christian, Formalist, and Hypocrisy soon arrive at the foot of the *Hill Difficulty*. Three pilgrims, three decisions.

  Formalist, facing the steepness of the Hill Difficulty, chooses the path to the left around the mountain. The path is named *Danger*. Its name indicates that this is not the straight way but is a way of great variety and many religious philosophies.

  Hypocrisy, seeing that the Hill Difficulty will require more commitment than he is willing to make, chooses the path to the right, a path named *Destruction*. This pathway also represents a way that is not the straight way, also a way with a wide variety of many other religious and social philosophies.

  Danger and Destruction together represent all the ways that are not the straight way, the righteous way, the Lord's way. Today they might be the ways of Socialism, New Age religions, prosperity teachings, Darwinism, Fascism, Capitalism, Self-enlightenment, materialism, hedonism, Communism, Humanism, asceticism, or anything that is not the Lord's way. These all look like shortcuts, but the end result is utter and complete destruction of the soul.

8. Running, then walking, and finally crawling, Christian arrives at a place that is meant to be a temporary resting place. Here he stops and begins to read the *scroll* for encouragement and considers the *coat* given to him. He begins to contemplate the grace he has received in the middle of great difficulties. He reviews the precious promises of God in the middle of his struggles. And then he falls into a deep sleep. The simple lesson here is that a respite should never turn into a place of retirement. God gives us seasons of rest so we can gain the refreshment needed to push forward and strive with all our might toward the prize. A simple rest can become a long slumber, which may turn into a habitual lifestyle of self-indulgence and shirking. The result is the loss of the scroll, which represents a loss of assurance of salvation.

9. *Timorous* and *Mistrust* represent fair-weather pilgrims who are anxious to reach the Celestial City until they encounter persecution. The *lions* they report represent the wicked people of this world, animated by the wicked princes of the invisible realm who are dedicated to the destruction of anything genuinely godly, those who devise plans to obstruct the cause of Christ and His gospel from outside and from inside the visible church. They persecute the saints of God with whatever means they have at hand. In some ages they have been armed with the instruments of death. In other ages they can only intimidate and cause fear and confusion.

10. During this brief trial, Christian realizes that he has lost his *scroll*. In other words, he has lost his assurance of entering into the Celestial City. He painfully retraces his steps until he finds the scroll again. The cost of indolence and carelessness is driven hard and fast into the heart of Christian, who now is forced to travel over the same ground not once but three times.

11. Christian arrives at the *House Beautiful*, which represents the true church of Christ, whether it be stationed strategically in some large stone cathedral or in the humble home of a true believer.

12. The true Christian will persevere and move forward, even when filled with fear and trepidation. Christian comes close to the lions and is fearfully frozen for a moment. But then the *porter* of the House Beautiful, named *Watchful*, representing a church leader or pastor who shepherds believers through difficulty, encourages Christian to move forward without fear since the lions are chained. In other words, there was at that time a limit on the persecution of the true church of Christ. While persecution was frightening, sometimes leading to imprisonment and financial ruin, it was rarely deadly in Bunyan's day if one kept to the path. Other generations of Christians were not so fortunate, although in the end those who have suffered deadly persecution for the sake of the gospel will be favored by the Lord.

13. Five people who question the legitimacy of his Christian testimony now interview Christian. Watchful inquires regarding his beliefs and his experience. *Discretion*,

Prudence, *Piety*, and *Charity* all take slightly different paths of investigation. Christian is approved, and all deem his testimony genuine. His admittance into the true church of Christ is based on regeneration, not merely on an affirmation of a creed or doctrine. The new convert is tested to see if the words he professes are justified with corresponding fruit in his life. Christian's testimony has all the earmarks of an authentic conversion, and the church receives him joyfully.

14. Christian is armed for the battle ahead, all through the testimony of God's Word. The preeminent job of the church is to equip Christian for life's challenges. This requires the emphasis on being fitted with tested armor. He is tutored in the Word of God. He is encouraged to rely on the Lord alone through faith in His promises and providence. He is drilled in the doctrines of salvation and is encouraged to allow these truths to work themselves deep into his soul. He is encouraged to live righteously by having within him a righteous mind soaked in Scripture and demonstrated in right living. He is taught how to pray. He is encouraged to share his faith with those who do not have peace with God.

Chapter Four: A Fierce Battle and a Dark Valley

1. Christian is immediately put to the test by the foul fiend *Apollyon*, who is the Destroyer. Christian is about to go through a process of intense humiliation. First he is encouraged to give up his pilgrimage by a series of arguments meant to shame and discourage him; then he is enticed to retreat by the powers of intimidation and accusations. When Apollyon cannot re-conquer Christian by defeating him with strategic discussion and attacking his mind, he becomes sensual and carnal in his attacks. Apollyon's true nature emerges without any further charade as he continues the attack, provoked by his hatred for the King of the Highway.

2. Christian receives many wounds and stumbles backwards as he struggles with his own imperfections and remaining unbelief. He despairs as he is tested beyond his limits, but God intervenes. The Word of God is freshly and graciously put within Christian's mind, and believing these truths with renewed faith he is spared again by God's grace alone.

3. The Word of God gives wounded Christian the victory. God renews his hope with His own promises, and Christian gives the Destroyer a deadly thrust resulting in a mortal wound to the enemy of the pilgrim's soul. Christian on his own could not defeat Apollyon. The sword of the Word of God is the only instrument that can accomplish such a task.

4. Christian may have entered the Valley of Humiliation overconfident and puffed up with false pride, but he departs with humble reliance on the Word of God and prayerful gratitude to the Lord of the Highway who has come to his aid and saved him from the Destroyer. He goes forward with his sword drawn. He has learned his lesson and now relies consciously on God's Word for protection.

5. No sooner has Christian departed from the Valley of Humiliation than he enters *the Valley of the Shadow of Death*. This represents the counterpoint to all the excitement of the conflict in the Valley of Humiliation. It is a place of depression and solitude. It is a dark place full of moody and morbid thoughts. Everything that accompanies death fills the atmosphere of this place and stifles the soul with darkness. It is the primer for Hell, a foretaste of the doom that awaits the unfaithful and unbelieving. Everything in this place cries out in protest against the best hopes and aspirations of a believer. Why is it necessary for Christian to pass through this dismal valley?

   This place is meant for Christian's growth, although at the time it is hard to see the purpose of such a place. It is always hard to see the purpose in wilderness wanderings until after they are over.

6. Christian meets two *men* who report to Christian that they have given up the pilgrimage to the Celestial City and are fleeing for their lives, in the face of hobgoblins, dragons, satyrs, unspeakable misery, howling, yelling, and other unspeakable horrors. They

are like the ten spies who returned to the children of Israel with an evil report about the Land of Promise. They are motivated by what they see and what they hear and are not persuaded of better things by the Word of God. Their final punishment will be the very misery they seek to avoid. The final end of a Christian will be peace and security, no matter what temporary trials lay just ahead.

7. We should not take lightly the horrible thoughts this place of death and destruction are meant to unveil. We are warned about the misery of death and Hell and should reflect upon its timeless torments and endless darkness in which men grope hopelessly for some relief that they are fully persuaded no longer exists.

8. Christian is certainly not unaffected by this gloomy, depressing, and frightening place, but he is determined to move through it with great care.

9. Christian chooses his steps carefully, as there was a deep *ditch* on his right side and a very dangerous *quagmire* on his left. The ditch on his right side represents error in doctrine. The quagmire on his left side represents the danger of moral failings.

10. Christian comes to the very mouth of *Hell* where he is forced to seriously consider the plight of the damned. It is here that Christian feels himself overwhelmed by all the demons of Hell. He feels fear, as he believes the devils are drawing nearer, but it is a fear that causes reflection and ultimately his defiant proclamation, *"I will walk in the strength of the Lord God."* Only then do the enemies retreat.

11. A new day comes, and with it Christian is able to clearly see the perils and hazards he has passed through. The new light also gives Christian much to be thankful for, as he views ahead with clear vision the second half of his journey. It is filled with pits and snares, traps and other perils that would have made safe passage in the dark almost impossible. This is a picture of God's perfectly timed mercies, without which no pilgrim would ever safely complete the journey.

Chapter Five: A Faithful Friend

1. Christian is about to experience fellowship with *Faithful*. The faith and hope they hold in common draws them together in a lifelong relationship. Faithful and Christian are very different in a number of ways. Faithful represents a simple, more common man than Christian. He is less complicated, less fearful, and more humble. The carnal traps of this world tempt Faithful, while Christian is more easily bent toward morbid fearfulness about his own guilt. Faithful receives the promises of God without staggering at them and thereby escapes being mired in the Swamp of Despond. But he does confess to being tempted by *Madam Wanton*, revealing a more base nature. Apollyon does not attack Faithful, but Faithful is troubled by the appeals of *Discontent* and *Shame* whose attack is aimed at his abandonment of more conventional mores.

   Christian and Faithful face different challenges and difficulties in this life, Bunyan's way of kindly reminding us that God's children are not stamped out of a cookie cutter, nor are they all equally tempted and tested in the same way. They are united by the fact that they are sinners saved by grace, but the application of grace upon the hearts of men is efficient no matter how different are the scars and weaknesses that sin has shaped in the individual heart.

2. The friendship between Christian and Faithful is sealed with a helping compassionate hand, which reminds us that many of the stumbles in life are preceded by pride and vainglory, and this is precisely when the helping firm hand of friendship and concern is the most needed.

3. Faithful and Christian have at the very root of their friendship a common story of receiving grace and mercy. The textures of both testimonies are meant to intertwine, encourage, and instruct. Both pilgrims learn valuable lessons as they recount to each other the distinctive experiences that bring both personal and common enlightenment and blessing. Declaring what God has done in the soul is the common ground that unites all Christians, no matter their background. This fellowship that has at its base

the wonder and constant amazement at the gracious provision and mercy of God is unique to Christians, and proof of hearts that have been humbled by grace and rightly motivated by a wholesome fear of the Lord. The exercise is soothing, refreshing, instructive, and beneficial to both pilgrims. It is also Bunyan's way of rehearsing the basic principles of Christian discipleship and biblical truth.

4. Faithful is also a reminder of how important companionship is to the Christian walk, but not more important than the desire for eternal life that motivated Faithful to keep fleeing for his life, no matter how strong the desire for friendship.

Chapter Six: A Faith Beyond Words

1. *Talkative* represents the man or woman who delights in talking about divine things but has only theoretical knowledge of such things. No actual personal heart experience correlates to the matters they love to discuss so eloquently. They are often highly esteemed by others, but those closest to them would quickly betray a life out-of-sync with their words. The mask fashioned by fluency with all subjects divine hides their real life.

2. Talkative is not easily unmasked since he loves to discuss all that is good, biblical, and supernatural. Faithful, the less discriminating of the two genuine pilgrims, is at first taken in by the silky words and orthodoxy of Talkative. But after a little instruction by Christian, Faithful investigates the life of Talkative more closely. Once the layers of religious talk are peeled off, the exposed surface turns out to be unmarked by any genuine repentance. Talkative in the end is all vaporous talk, coexisting with a life that is unconverted and graceless.

   There is a warning here for true pilgrims. Beware of the talker, but also be careful not to judge too quickly those whom God has blessed with both genuine grace and a fluency to speak of divine mercy in ways more eloquent than others. The proof is in the life—not a perfect life, but a life that both delights in divine truth and magnifies God, the only giver of the sovereign grace that always produces the truly fruitful, fragrant life.

3. Bunyan helps us further shape the character of Talkative when he tell us that he lives in *Prating-Row* with his father *Say-well*. The entire family's reputation is one of spiritual impoverishment in which there is much talk about working for the Kingdom, while nothing is actually ever accomplished. The theoretical talk is one dimension that is in constant contrast and disharmony with the behavior. The real life of Talkative is a display of brutishness, ruthlessness, stinginess, and dishonesty. The bothersome noise of religious talk grows irksome when laid upon the living score of discordant behavior. Talkative's life can be read with little confusion when the high-sounding rhetoric is set alongside the double-dealing, deceitful, self-centered, and abusive behavior that litters the path down which he has trod.

4. The conversation between Faithful and Talkative ends when Faithful challenges Talkative to show in his life the fruits of the truths he so easily talks about. This conversation exposes the matter, and the false pilgrim is soon separated from the true pilgrim.

   To cry out against sin but to tolerate it comfortably in the heart is an equation that sums up the false pretense of Talkative. The work of grace in the heart offers proofs that cannot be denied. The eloquent Talkative simply lacks the experiential work of grace in his heart.

   Again, Christians should be warned not to judge too quickly, since many Christians struggle with sin and surrender in the battlefield of life and often fail. The important thing to understand is that God will always produce a fruitful life in those He has conquered and occupies. The same Lord will disqualify those whose religion is only talk by ordaining that their life lacks the abundance of genuine good fruit while bad fruit abounds.

5. Christian and Faithful who are now passing through a *wilderness* are left alone to continue encouraging each other. What Bunyan may have in mind is a sense of dryness and

discouragement that comes after any lengthy encounter with ones such as Talkative. After all was said, it was a dry and weary experience. Dry conversation depresses the soul.

Chapter Seven: On Trial for the Gospel

1. *Evangelist* returns to the sides of the two pilgrims both to investigate and to encourage them to faithfully endure what lies ahead.
2. Evangelist is pictured as an astute doctor of the soul. His pastoral inquiries are motivated by a genuine interest in the well-being of the two pilgrims, and his duty is to warn and instruct them as they make the treacherous journey to the Celestial City. He is joyful about their achievements and adds perspective to their trials, which are meant to both strengthen and humble the two pilgrims.
3. His basic message is meant to put steel in their backbone and to encourage them to run the race and seek the prize of Heaven. He comes to remind them that they have an enemy who seeks to destroy them.
4. Ahead, warns Evangelist, lies *Vanity Fair*. It is a place they must go through, although dangers and tribulation await all pilgrims who enter. And, prophesies Evangelist, one of them will arrive at the Celestial City before the other. Evangelist directs Christian's and Faithfull's gaze toward the incorruptible crown that is set before them.
5. Christian and Faithful have fled the City of Destruction, only to now enter Vanity Fair. What is the difference? The answer is that Christian and Faithful have changed. They now see with Heaven's eyes the schemes, traps, enticements, and entertainments of the world in a new way. So far the journey has brought us into individual contact with the likes of Mr. Worldly-Wiseman, Obstinate, Pliable, and Madam Wanton. Now Christian and Faithful must encounter the corporate system that animates all the forces who would block the progress of a true pilgrim bound for the Celestial City. Vanity Fair is the City of Destruction, the world, dressed in its best party dress. It is the place where the most seductive attractions of the world take center stage in an attempt to steal our gaze, cool our resolve, and shake our confidence, which is to be in the God who is the maker and builder of the yet unseen city.
6. In Vanity Fair live the broad-minded, who hate the narrow and old-fashioned. It is a place where Christians are invited to rest from what is commonly seen as the over-stringent demands of Jesus Christ, where Christians are lulled into ever more carnal amusements. All of these distractions are meant to dull the sense of sin and seduce the pilgrim into becoming lukewarm in both his confession and his walk. Making concessions to sin in Vanity Fair is applauded as a sign of maturity and a pre-condition of fellowship and acceptance.

   Everything in Vanity Fair is designed to detour the journey to the Celestial City by whatever means are most agreeable to the fallen heart of man. If pandering does not work, then direct attacks will accomplish the same thing in Vanity Fair.
7. No longer bewitched by the seductive enticements of Vanity Fair, *Hopeful* is convinced of the gospel's truth because of Christian and Faithful's behavior and testimony while under severe persecution. He then joins Christian on his pilgrimage. Is it not a strange matter that out of all the torment, maligning, and martyrdom designed to overwhelm and destroy Faithful, Hopeful emerges? Hopeful is first and foremost the product of the genuine testimony of the two other pilgrims. Secondly, he is the picture of his very name, Hopeful. The gospel produces hope.

Chapter Eight: Confronting Worldly Attachments

1. As Christian and Hopeful begin their journey together, they soon meet up with a character who will not immediately divulge his name. He is in fact ashamed of his name because it identifies him with the world, and he has not been able to obtain a new name, which would recommend him as a genuine pilgrim.

2. *By-ends*, we learn, is from the town of *Fair-speech* and is a nephew of *Rev. Two-tongues*. By-ends by his own confession is schooled in religious duplicity and exists on the edges of the religious establishment best known for its modern, nuanced views that keep it safe with the world while pretending to have religious affections.

3. By-ends represents the kind of man who has lifted himself up through craft and manipulation, loves all that is sophisticated and refined, and uses his religious affiliation to advance his own career. His earthy bank account is all that matters. He has no account in Heaven and no checkbook backed by true faith upon which to draw.

4. By-ends is a religious charlatan whose only purpose is to aggrandize himself, guard his worldly reputation, and gain as much vainglory as this world has to offer. He is the personification of evil motives wrapped in the robe of good intentions and charitable causes, a double-minded man.

5. The introduction of *Mr. Hold-the world*, *Mr. Money-love*, and *Mr. Save-all*, whose names describe them without need for further explanation, round out the picture of the fashionable religious frauds that should be avoided by true pilgrims at all costs.

Chapter Nine: Refreshment at God's River

1. Christian and Hopeful retire to a plain called *Ease* where *Demas*, the mine-keeper, attempts to persuade them to turn out of the way to mine for silver. Great wealth for little effort is promised. Demas represents the temptation to make a lifestyle of covetousness while still holding religious convictions. It is the idea that you can hold on to comfort and self-satisfaction in one hand with your religious principles balanced nicely in the other.

2. By-Ends, Demas, and the salt pillar of Lot's wife provide a trilogy of warnings against the perils of loving this world.

Chapter Ten: Prisoners of Despair

1. Christian, who showed good judgment in his encounter with By-ends, carelessly slips over into *By-Path Meadow* to avoid the rocky path leading to the Celestial City. What starts out as a thoughtless accommodation to sore feet and the desire to avoid small difficulties ends in near-tragedy.

2. It is not an accident that just before Christian rediscovers the *key called Promise*, Hopeful glimmers with new hope. This prompts Christian to remember how faithfully and lovingly God has preserved him in the past.

   In our own circumstances, the first steps back from our doubt and despair are often gilded with the memories of how God has preserved us and kept us in the past. He who began the good work, will He not finish it? Oh, yes, a thousand times yes!

3. *Giant Despair*, his wife *Distrust*, and *Doubting Castle* can all be understood in light of the key called Promise. That key represents all the promises of God directed toward sinners who belong to His Son. But in a broader light, these promises are all God's good plans for fallen sinners revealed in His Word. In a practical sense this key epitomizes all the promises that the Holy Spirit has deposited into the heart and mind of a Christian. When a Christian devalues, ignores, depresses, or otherwise despises by neglect the sure promises of God, the seeds of doubt find a welcome place to ripen into all sorts of toxic and malicious fruit. For some it is doubts about being God's elect; for others it is the tormenting thought that they are no longer able to receive God's mercy; others begin to question God's motives and character. At the extreme, some even entertain thoughts of suicide in order to escape the overwhelming cloud of anguish and hopelessness enveloping them. All these conditions and a thousand more are symptoms that can overtake us when we ignore or neglect the mighty promises of God and His great goodness while seeking ease from the many challenges of the narrow path. God is to be worshiped, not our doubts and fears. Our doubts and fears are to be overcome by the good and sure Word of God.

Chapter Eleven: Shepherds' Warnings, Dangers Avoided

1. The *Delectable Mountains* are a type of the church, which can only be appreciated after the experiential development of spiritual maturity.

2. The shepherds are pastors, and the pastoral gifts are represented by their names *Watchful*, *Experience*, *Sincere*, and *Knowledge*. The gardens, vineyards, fountains, and bountifully textured terrain are metaphors for the richness of spirit that comes with experience in the Christian walk. They also describe the contemplation of heavenly delights that are shadows of the splendor just ahead.

3. The Delectable Mountains represent the comfort of the local church and also the place where true pilgrims are constantly cautioned about the perils that lie ahead. The *hill called Error*, *the mountain called Caution*, Doubting Castle, the *byway to Hell*, and finally the hill called *Clear* are all metaphors designed to both caution and to give hope to weary pilgrims.

   The Delectable Mountains are also the place where Christians may reflect on past perils and on the goodness of God whose saving hand has plucked them from the pitfalls that have assailed them in the past. What better place to contemplate both the goodness and severity of the gospel.

4. The respite in the Delectable Mountains concludes with special sendoffs from the shepherds. One encouraged them to heed the exposition of God's Word by God's faithful ministers, as pictured by *a map of the way*. The second warned the pilgrims to beware of the *Flatterer*—a picture of all that deludes us and appeals to our vanity. The third warned against falling asleep on the *Enchanted Ground*. This is a constant reminder that we need to humbly keep watch over our own souls. The great danger in this place is the gradual and almost imperceptible temptation to slumber and become drowsy in the care of our heart and soul. The fourth shepherd bid them Godspeed, a genuine prayer for both safety and a speedy journey to the Celestial City.

Chapter Twelve: Faith under Attack

1. Upon continuing the pilgrimage, Christian and Hopeful soon meet *Ignorance* from the country of *Conceit*. Since the opposite of ignorance is knowledge, and the opposite of conceit is humility, an important point is about to be made. But first it must be understood that Bunyan has in mind a certain type of ignorance.

   It is not an all-pervasive ignorance, as illustrated by newborn chicks that carry around with them on their heads the blinding half shell out of which they were born. Bunyan is not alluding to the ignorance of the inexperienced or dull-minded person but rather a very specific self-willed ignorance—a deliberate and willful ignorance of the saving gospel truths.

2. Bunyan shows allegorically the complete blindness and particular ignorance of the false pilgrim who seems headed for the Celestial City, ignorance buffered and encapsulated with pride and conceit. This ignorance is unassailable and cannot be penetrated with the truths of the Holy Scriptures.

3. Ignorance represents the condition of one of the largest groups of false pilgrims. This malady can be diagnosed by its outcome in the deeds and words of those afflicted. The ignorant have no need to ask directions or ever feel a twinge of doubt about their condition. Ignorance holds to everything that is good and has convinced himself of the merits of his deeds and the personal goodness of his character. As such, his journey out of the country of Conceit is not motivated by thoughts of destruction or judgment but rather the desire to exchange a good place for a better one. For Ignorance, the journey from Conceit to the Celestial City is like a pleasant walk in the park, with grassy knolls and soft turf underfoot.

   We must rely only on Christ who died to deliver us from the wrath of God. It is He alone who secures us to a life that is eternal with Him. It is Christ alone in our hearts who produces humility, deep contrition, and unspeakable joy. It is Christ in us who is constantly disqualifying our pride and conceit and helps us see them as the filthy rags they are. It is through Christ that all our knowledge has its full and complete purpose. Christ alone!

4. Next we meet *Turn-Away*. After exploring the confident Ignorance, we are now directed to consider the false pilgrim in the *dark lane*. Clearly *dark lane* is a metaphor for an unenlightened soul.

5. Turn-Away is considered to be a nominal Christian, but when stripped of his exterior religiosity and piety, what lies behind the mask is an apostate, ungodly, and disloyal pilgrim who has abandoned his previous gospel confession. The fickleness and abandonment are not meant to convey the loss of true gospel conviction but rather the fact that it was never present. This is a soul that has never been illuminated by the Holy Spirit, and in the end we see hellish spirits who are about to claim their prize and occupy the temple of this poor soul. Beware of gospel pretense!

6. We are meant to compare *Little-Faith* with Turn-Away. Little-Faith is the picture of a true but sadly weak Christian. Close examination of this character is meant to caution us about making too harsh a judgment about the Christian who has found himself suffering the consequences of a weak faith, guilt, and unbelief. He is the picture of the Christian who fails to be alert and watchful, is allured by the ways of the world, and falls under the tyranny and into the traps of Satan.

7. Little-Faith loses his courage to *Faint-Heart*, is robbed by *Mistrust*, and is clubbed nearly to death by *Guilt*. The lesson is clear, and the outcome seems certain. Everything points to the total abandonment that comes with mistrust and the loss of Heaven.

8. Our salvation, for those who have come the way of the cross to Christ, is sealed by the Holy Spirit. Those redeemed by a sinless substitute may at times lose all self-confidence and may on occasion feel themselves stumbling hopelessly into *Dead Man's Lane*. The sword of protection is lost, the breastplate of righteousness battered, the shield of faith knocked from our trembling hands and unreachable, the helmet of salvation sideways on our head restricting all vision. In a word, we may find ourselves altogether hopeless.

But wait! One promise remains unassailable by the enemies of our soul. One promise is far out of our enemies' reach and towers over them like a mighty fortress. Only one promise is left, but that promise is good enough! The Lord of the Highway who has begun a good work in the soul of even the weakest, most crippled pilgrim will *never* abandon him to the enemy. Little-Faith belonged to the King, and the King is greater than all the enemies of our soul combined. He will never leave us or forsake us. In this we can have *Good Confidence* and *Great-Grace* that is greater than all our sins. Little-Faith is miraculously rescued, as are we all, by the matchless grace of God.

9. Some few may confidently march up to the gates of the Celestial City and be welcomed with much joy. Others may feebly and haltingly approach the same gate overcome with the true sense of their failings and infirmities. But for them the gates will also open, and all the tears will turn to unending praise for the Christ who came to save unworthy sinners.

We are warned by the story of Little-Faith to stay alert and vigilant, but also to remain humble. The story of Little-Faith could just as easily be our story. We should avoid any self-confidence or vain pride in our spiritual accomplishments. These achievements are *jewels* that remain in our possession only by the grace of God. Comparing ourselves confidently to the sorry likes of Little-Faith may soon cause our own humiliating defeat. As Jesus told Peter in Luke 22:31–32 (*English Standard Version*), "Simon, Simon, behold, Satan demanded to have you that he might sift you like wheat, but I have prayed for you that your faith may not fail." Our confidence must remain exclusively in the Lord!

10. Christian and Hopeful have theologically solved the problem of Little-Faith and tested the testimony of Ignorance. Nevertheless Hopeful has bouts with smugness, while Christian becomes testy and a little arrogant in his treatment of Hopeful.

Chapter Thirteen: Flattering Enemies and Renewed Trust

1. What follows now is instructive. It is often when considering the failings of others that we come the closest to failing ourselves. While congratulating ourselves for our orthodoxy and spiritual discernment, we can easily wander ever so slightly off the straight path. *The Flatterer* appears in robes of light, is disingenuously full of congratulations for the good and steady progress made by Christian and Hopeful, and offers to guide them to the Celestial City.

2. The Flatterer is a picture of a smooth-talking false teacher. He is sly and deceptive, easily taking Christian and Hopeful on a meandering path that is meant to distance them from the Celestial City. All this is birthed by spiritual pride.

3. The *net* represents teachings not in line with Scripture. The litany of false teachings that are ensnaring mature Christian pilgrims has grown in these last days.

4. Christian and Faithful now meet *Atheist*. The most important thing to notice about Atheist is that *"his back [is] toward Zion."* The second thing we notice is the mocking laughter and belittling attitude toward anything but the tiny material world he has circumscribed with his small sensual mind. Atheist is the type that despises the Bible and the faith and hope it produces. He doesn't understand those sinners who have had the Son of God and His gracious purpose revealed to them in the pages of that most royal book.

5. Atheist is the naturalist, the humanist, the Darwinist, the scientist of unbelief, and the blasphemer. He represents that class of men that has been well instructed in the unbelief of the world and holds to it firmly and boastfully.

6. Atheist has a superior and callous spirit, always ready to debate and rebuke those of faith. His contempt for the unseen world is great and fixed. Any word of faith or hope unleashes in him a barrage of filthy bombast and prideful pronouncements. He is intolerant of anything that is spiritual and contemptuous of anyone whose faith directs them to the Celestial City. He is the very picture of the false professors who teach nothing but a hopeless, deterministic naturalism.

7. Christian soon produces the best remedy for such fellows as the self-worshiping Atheist. Distance is the remedy, and the more of it, the greater the wisdom. A word of reason is given to Atheist, the reason for the hope that presses them forward to the Celestial City. But once given, the heavenward mind should quickly seek to be about the journey toward Heaven, unbothered by the foolishness of all those who say there is no God. God is not glorified by anyone who makes an idol of unbelief and is certainly not going to promote in his true pilgrims the temptation to judge between our doubts, whether homegrown or imported from the University of Atheism, and his most Holy and Glorious Person. Let God be God and every man a liar!

8. Next we travel across the *Enchanted Ground*. This represents those periods of temporary peace and tranquility in our pilgrimage that are meant to enlarge our capacity to contemplate on the goodness of God. This time often results in the relaxation of spiritual effort, resulting in unholy indulgences and ultimately in a disability of our spiritual health, or worse. The signs that one is falling asleep on the plains of the Enchanted Ground are lukewarmness, inactivity, spiritual laziness, slothfulness, and sinking into doctrinal simplemindedness—in a word, slumbering while the spiritual house so patiently and painfully constructed burns down around one's ears.

9. This anecdote pictures vigorous interaction with spiritual truth, especially those truths that warn and caution us to run the race with patience and endurance. We are to keep awake with lively thoughts of the loving-kindness of our Lord and to keep strong ties with men and women who are the most likely to encourage and strengthen our faith, while avoiding the sleeping saints who seem to be able to snooze in a hurricane and sleep through an earthquake.

10. Recount the journey of God's special goodness to you on your pilgrimage to the Celestial City. "Awake, my soul, awake and hear my Savior's plea. Come to the living fountain and drink large drafts of the Savior."

Chapter Fifteen: Home in the Celestial City

1. On the horizon is *Beulah Land* with all its sweet and pleasant delights. Beulah Land is beyond the dark reach of all ill places, which are now simply faded, muted memories. What the Christian now affirms is God's keeping power and love for poor pilgrims.

2. This most wonderful place is where the sunshine appears to lighten the pilgrims' earthly concerns and illuminate the destination lying just ahead. Heaven's lights now beckon with a simple power that draws the soul into an indescribable panting for Paradise. This is the place where the final groaning—the constant noise of this temporal existence—is made silent by the unspeakable light and life that emanates from the shining city, whose maker and builder is God. Just a few breaths more of this temporal air, and soon the lungs will be filled with the light-infused atmosphere of the Celestial City.

3. Beulah Land is that place reserved for every Christian just before he enters the Celestial City, although many forego the glorious experience for reasons of spiritual destitution. But for the seasoned pilgrim in the sunset of his pilgrimage, Beulah Land looms lush and large with spiritual and heavenly graces.

4. This is blood-bought expectation, glory-filled anticipation, and Spirit-sealed transportation to a better country. Here all your desires are to do what will make you most ravenously happy, to glorify God with a new heart, your focus now fixed on the One whose wounds have certified your passage to Heaven. Heaven is Christ, and Christ is Heaven!

5. Without any thought of future difficulties, Christian and Hopeful seem ready to climb toward the Celestial City. With a zealous sense of their own sufficiency they move toward the Celestial City and the River of Death.

6. It is easy for us to forget that the last great enemy is death. All the vain methods to try and gloss over this great opponent are simply vain and unhelpful. We should not deceive ourselves as to the ferociousness of this last and final obstacle to the soul. Death *is* the final enemy.

7. We should not think that death will be free from trouble or pain. God is faithful in the deaths that are painless and peaceful, as well as in the ones that are full of final suffering and horror. The true believer has no guarantee that his death will be a painless slipping away. It may be anything but painless. Death is the last trial, and for some the experience will be a horrific affliction, while for others it may be a quick and relatively painless departure. In either case we can trust that the God who raised Jesus from the dead is the same God who will deliver us.

8. We who observe death will one day be called to encounter the final enemy with no way of escape, unless the Lord comes first. Christian gives us all hope that even in the River of Death, when thoughts of our own unrighteousness overwhelm and assail us for the last time, though we seem to almost drown in hopelessness, we are not without comfort or assistance.

   Death is not a shallow trickling stream over which we can leap with light-footed abandon. Death is a meandering, dark, and sometimes treacherous river that seeks at every turn to interfere with our future hope. Death is the last chasm over which the soul must cross. It is the end of this life and all the hopes and dreams of this life. For those who have only dreamed dreams of this life, death is a stunning and fearful place unlike any other. No wonder the world so willfully ignores or shrouds death in fanciful language in its attempt to render it obscure and benign. We should not expect to escape the fear that death brings, but we may expect to meet those fears with faith as God gives it.

   Christian faces death with despair and great anxiety, as Satan and his own memory of past sins flood his mind for the final attack on his soul. Christian finds the waters chilling, deep, and treacherous, slipping beneath them with despondency, only to be lifted up by God's gentle but firm grace.

   When all seems lost, the Lord Himself through the testimony of Hopeful firmly but gently reminds Christian that he is redeemed, called by His name, that God is present in his circumstances and able to save to the utmost.

Hopeful approaches death with more cheer and courage. For him the final journey as he walks through on firm ground is less sorrowful and more peaceful.

Likewise, we should not forget Faithful whose journey through the dark river was glorious.

9. Earlier in his journey, when Pliable asked, "What company shall we have in the Celestial City?" Christian, who with little light and only an inkling of the realities of Heaven, had proclaimed, "We will be with seraphim and cherubim and creatures who will dazzle your eyes when you look at them. You will meet with thousands who have gone before us to that place. None of them are hurtful, but all of them are loving and holy, every one walking in the sight of God and standing in His presence with acceptance forever. In a word, there we will see the elders with their golden crowns. There we will see the holy virgins with their golden harps. There we will see men who were cut in pieces by the world, burnt in flames, eaten by beasts, drowned in the seas, suffering all this and more for the love they have for the Lord of the place. Everyone in that place is clothed with immortality, as with a robe."

10. Finally we are shown the frightening and sobering conclusion of the life of Ignorance. This dreary picture of Ignorance being cast into Hell is meant to add a final caution and warning to all who would seek the Celestial City. Heaven is not for everyone. It is not for those who, like Ignorance, have rejected the true gospel and substituted a gospel of self-righteousness and personal attainment. If you remain self-sufficient, then you have no hope of being received into the Celestial City but should expect Hell as your final destination.

Hell is a shocking and unpopular topic for Christians in this present age. It is no accident that Bunyan concludes *The Pilgrim's Progress* with this sobering warning to the unbeliever.

As certainly as there is a Heaven, there is a Hell. A Hell to be avoided at all costs. All worldly enterprises, ventures, trophies, offices, lands, riches, accomplishments, accommodations, powers, entertainments, applause, approval, and vanities turn to dust when weighed against the prospect of Heaven.

Finally, for those who ignore the proclamation of the gospel, a Christless eternity in Hell awaits them as certainly as God's Word is always true. Bunyan's final word is a carbon copy of our Lord's word. Repent and believe! Believe the gospel of Jesus Christ!

May you be a true pilgrim with a courageous testimony that Christ was crucified for sinners and is their Savior.

Our hope is Christ, our narrow but sure path to the Celestial City. Seek no other!